Happy Bi[rthday]
25 Successful Years.
Hope there are many more.
Best Wishes
Anne Mather

Dear Reader,

Happy twenty-fifth birthday, Harlequin Presents®. We've grown up together because I've been a keen romance reader since my teens. I enjoy reading romance every bit as much as I enjoy writing it. It was an incredible thrill to have my first book published in 1987, and I still feel privileged when I see my books for sale. When I'm telling their stories, my heroes and heroines are as real to me as my own family. I hope Rosie and Constantine seem as real to you.

Lynne Graham

Lynne Graham

LYNNE GRAHAM

The Secret Wife

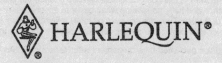

HARLEQUIN®

TORONTO · NEW YORK · LONDON
AMSTERDAM · PARIS · SYDNEY · HAMBURG
STOCKHOLM · ATHENS · TOKYO · MILAN · MADRID
PRAGUE · WARSAW · BUDAPEST · AUCKLAND

ISBN 0-373-11961-5

THE SECRET WIFE

First North American Publication 1998.

Copyright © 1997 by Lynne Graham.

Printed in U.S.A.

CHAPTER ONE

HER heart beating like a drum, Rosie crept into the church when the rush was over, sliding into a pew near the back to listen to the memorial service from a safe distance. Anton Estrada had been well-known in the city of London. The dim interior was crammed to capacity with those who wished to pay their last respects.

A black gold-embroidered scarf covering her bowed head, Rosie shivered, lost in the dark well of her grief. As far back as she could remember she had been alone, but for a few agonisingly brief months she had had Anton. And now he was gone, that warm, laughing man, who had called her the joy he had waited for all his life and the greatest love of his existence. Tears shimmering in her shadowed green eyes, she stared down at the huge ornate emerald on her finger until it blurred out of focus. Well, who would love her now? she thought painfully. Who indeed would ever love her like that again?

The silence and the soft murmur of voices finally penetrated. In a daze, she glanced up and realised that the service was over and the church was almost empty again. Disconcerted by her loss of concentration, she flew upright and headed for the exit. A corner of her scarf caught on the end of a pew, jerking her head back, making her stumble.

She would have fallen but for the strong, masculine hand that came out of nowhere to close round her slender forearm and steady her. 'Are you all right?' a dark, honey-rich drawl enquired and her lush dark lashes fluttered in momentary bemusement as the fleeting familiarity of accented English washed over her and filled her with unbelievable pain. 'Perhaps you should sit down again—'

'No...' Riven with tension, Rosie straightened and broke free of that male grasp. Forgetting that her scarf was caught, she barely felt the pull as it trailed off and freed the wild, tumbling mass of her Titian hair from confinement. Involuntarily, she glanced up and froze in stark horror, her breath snarled up in her throat, her beautiful face stiffening like pale, tear-streaked marble into stricken stillness. Sheer shock slowed her heartbeat to a numbing thud that echoed sickly in her eardrums.

Constantine Voulos stared down at her, apparently entrapped by the same immobility that paralysed her. He *was* gorgeous, even more gorgeous than he had looked in Anton's photographs, Rosie registered helplessly. Luxuriant black hair, stunning bone structure and a wide, wickedly sensual mouth. A wave of dizziness engulfed her as she collided with mesmeric dark deep-set eyes. Her bemused gaze locked with compulsive intensity to his. It was as terrifying as walking off a cliff-edge and falling...and falling...and falling. She couldn't breathe and she couldn't speak. It panicked her.

'Who are you?' he murmured thickly, in one fluid movement drawing closer again as he tugged her scarf free and extended it to her.

Rosie turned white as death and backed off on legs that were ready to buckle, a dark, ferocious wave of violent and confused emotion consuming her. Constantine Voulos, the child whom Anton and his Greek wife, Thespina, had raised as their own.

'Your scarf...'

Jerkily, reluctantly, she reached out to the child who had become a man. It was a mistake. He caught her thin, trembling fingers in his.

'*Please...*' Rosie gasped, attempting to break the connection, her slim body already twisting on the brink of flight, panic currenting through her.

'*Christos!*' Constantine vented in raw disbelief as he recognised the antique emerald adorning her hand. 'Where did you get that ring?'

Astonished recognition had made him temporarily loosen his grip. Rosie snatched her fingers back and raced down the steps. The wintry breeze caught her curling torrent of hair and the long, loose black coat, making them flow out behind her like wings as she broke through the lingering groups of people outside and flew across the busy road, indifferent to the screeching brakes and honking horns that accompanied her dangerous passage.

Rosie wandered one last time round the silent rooms. Without Anton's larger-than-life presence the pretty little house was an empty shell. Having eradicated every scrap of evidence that she had ever lived within these walls, she would slam the door behind her and walk back into her own world. It couldn't have lasted much longer anyway, she told herself.

She cherished her freedom, yet she had allowed Anton to clip her wings. He had stubbornly persuaded and pressurised and finally pleaded until she'd surrendered and moved in, willing to compromise, wanting to be what he wanted her to be if that pleased him... but always knowing that sooner or later she would be forced to rebel.

'I am an independent spirit,' she had said to him gently once.

'Your independence was forced on you and it was a most unnatural responsibility for a young girl to carry,' Anton had countered with staunch disapproval. 'You no longer need to bear that responsibility now that I am here.'

And she had laughed and argued but not very hard, wryly aware that he could not begin to understand the life she had led or the background she came from any more than she could really comprehend *his* and that it would upset him if she were too honest. So they had built a bridge across the great divide of wealth and culture by making careful allowances on both sides, and ironically it had been remarkably easy for right from the beginning there had been this amazing sense of mutual recognition.

She had been lucky to have that much, she reflected painfully. Four months of perfect happiness was more than some people achieved in a lifetime. Four months of being loved passionately, unconditionally, selflessly. Good memories had taken the edge off the bad ones. She swallowed the thickness of tears in her throat and smiled with sudden brilliance. Nobody could take those memories away. Or the ring that had been in the Estrada family for two centuries, the single surviving heirloom which Anton had slid onto her finger with unashamed tears in his dark eyes.

'Now it will be worn again for only now is it where it truly belongs.'

Rosie recalled Constantine's outraged incredulity when he had recognised that ring and a humourless laugh escaped her. So I accepted one little memento; think yourself lucky, Constantine Voulos, for had I been greedy I could have taken far more! Because Anton had wanted to lay the world at her feet. His joy and pride in her had dangerously overwhelmed every other loyalty. That was the only thing they had ever argued about.

And Rosie was guiltily conscious that it had been a struggle to keep her conscience in control. It hadn't been his wealth that had made her feel like that; she simply couldn't imagine *having* that kind of money. No, it had been the squirming attacks of resentment which she had fought to conceal, knowing just how much those feelings would have distressed him. But she was human, fallible, as capable as anyone else of thinking self-pitying thoughts and experiencing envy.

At the age of nine, Constantine Voulos had lost his parents in a car accident. Anton and Thespina had taken Constantine into their home and brought him up as if he were their own child. It had never occurred to Anton that Rosie might resent his constant references to his substitute son's innumerable virtues and talents, only to despise herself for the unreasoning injustice of such childish promptings.

The silence began to get to Rosie. She shivered at the echo of her own footsteps. She *should* have cleared out the day Anton had died but she had been in such shock she had simply stopped functioning. Only six weeks earlier, a mild heart attack had put him into hospital. She had been first at his bedside, reluctantly torn from him only when she'd realised that Thespina and Constantine were already on their way from the airport.

'Stay . . . to hell with them all!' Anton had grated recklessly, already inflamed by the nurse who had attempted to prevent her visit to his private room.

'You know you don't mean that. You can't do that to your wife,' Rosie had muttered tightly, her better self talking, her worse self bitter that she, who had more right than anyone, should have to fight her way in and then sneak her way out.

'You never use her name,' Anton had sighed heavily.

And she had flushed hotly, avoiding his gaze, too many complex emotions swirling about inside her, too much guilt, too much pain. Thespina had been his wife for over thirty years. A wonderfully loyal and loving wife, who had nonetheless been cruelly betrayed. And the simple fact that Thespina was unaware of that betrayal and indeed must be carefully protected from that knowledge did not make the brick-wall barrier of her very existence any more easy for Rosie to accept.

Rosie had slunk in and out of that hospital for an entire week, her natural buoyance soon reasserting itself to soothe her initially frantic fears about Anton's health. He was only fifty-five. He had been working too hard. Oh, they had talked endlessly about all the sensible things he would have to do in the future! It had occurred to neither of them that that future might be measured only in weeks.

He had taken a convalescent cruise round the Greek islands but on the same day that he'd flown back to London again Anton had had a massive heart attack. 'Gone within minutes!' his secretary had sobbed down the phone, still in shock. 'Who am I speaking to?' she had asked then for Rosie had never rung his office before, but when Anton had failed to meet her for lunch she had been worried sick.

Rosie had replaced the receiver in silence. Naturally she could not attend his funeral in Greece. Sick to the heart at her cruel exclusion, she had gone to the memorial service instead, only to run slap-bang into Constantine Voulos through her own clumsy lack of attention. That encounter yesterday had appalled Rosie. She should have packed her bags long ago and gone home! But she had wanted privacy in which to come to terms with the loss of the father she had known for so painfully short a time.

'Rosalie . . . ?'

Her heart lurched sickly against her breastbone, the oxygen locking at the foot of her convulsed throat. She jerked round in horror.

Constantine Voulos was standing on the landing outside her bedroom. He was breathing fast, his hard, strikingly handsome features set in a dark mask of fury as he moved towards her. 'That *is* your name, is it not?'

'What are you doing here?' Rosie gasped, her entire body turning cold and damp with instinctive fear. 'How did you get in?'

'You evil little vixen,' Constantine grated, his six-foot-three-inch all-male bulk blocking the doorway that was her only avenue of escape. He couldn't take his shimmering dark eyes off her. It was like being pinned to a wall by knives.

With enormous effort, Rosie straightened her slim shoulders and stood her ground but she was deathly pale. 'I don't know who you are or what you want—'

'You know exactly who I am!' Constantine slung at her, unimpressed, taking a frightening step closer.

'Stay away from me!' Rigid with tension, Rosie wondered frantically how he had found out about her and how much he knew.

'I wish I could... I really do wish that I could,' Constantine bit out with clenched fists, the explosive anger that emanated from him screaming along her nerve-endings like a violent storm warning.

Rosie retreated until the backs of her knees hit the divan bed. 'What do you w-want?'

'I want to wipe you off the face of this earth but I *cannot*... that is what inflames me! How did you persuade Anton to do something so insane?'

'Do... what?' she whispered blankly, too scared to be capable of rational thought.

'How did you persuade one of the most decent men I ever knew to sacrifice all honour and family loyalty?' Constantine seethed back at her.

'I don't know what you're talking about—'

'Don't you know what Anton did only days before his death?' Constantine demanded rawly, scanning the suitcase on the bed with a contemptuously curled lip. 'Have you any idea what his final words were before he died in my arms?'

Numbly, sickly, Rosie shook her head, a dense cloud of spiralling curls the colour of flames rippling round her rigid shoulders. She hadn't known that Constantine had been with her father when he died. Ironically that new knowledge brought a lump to her throat and warmed that cold place inside her as she thought of that dreadful day. Anton had not been alone but for his secretary. Constantine had been there, Constantine had been with him, and whether she liked it or not she knew just how much that would have meant to her father.

Constantine gave a great shout of raucous laughter that chilled her. Eyes black as night dug into her with unhidden repulsion. 'Every word which he struggled to speak related to *you!*'

'Oh...' Her stifled response barely broke the smouldering silence. And she heard his pain and didn't want to recognise it for what it was because she did not wish to admit that she could share *anything* with Constantine Voulos.

'He made me swear on my honour that I would protect you and respect his last wishes. But I didn't even know of your existence! I didn't understand who or even what he was referring to... nor did I know until last night *what* those last wishes were!' Constantine vented on another surge of barely contained rage that visibly tremored through his long, muscular length. 'He wrote a new will, and were it not for the fact that the publicity would destroy Thespina I would trail you through every court in Europe and crucify you for the greedy, calculating little vixen that you are before I would allow you to profit by a single drachma!'

'A *new* will?' Her teeth gritted as she withstood the lash of his insults. Hot, angry colour drove away her previous pallor. But at least she now understood what Constantine Voulos was doing here and why he was forcing such a confrontation. Evidently Anton had been foolish enough to leave her something in his will in spite of her fierce assurances that she wanted and needed nothing.

His nostrils flared as he surveyed her with dark fury. 'Months ago, Thespina suspected that there was another woman in his life. *Christos* ... I actually laughed when she shared her fears with me! I convinced her that it was only the excitement of a new business venture which was making Anton spend so much time in London. I was naïve indeed. I underestimated the lure of youth and beauty on even the most honourable of men. Anton was obsessed with you...he died with your name on his lips!'

'He loved me,' Rosie mumbled helplessly, the acid sting of tears burning behind her stricken eyes as she turned defensively away.

'And I would lay my life on the line before I would allow Thespina to endure that knowledge!' Constantine growled rawly.

She understood then. Evidently Constantine Voulos did *not* know who she was. He assumed that she was the other woman, Anton's mistress cosily set up in the proverbial love-nest. It was laughable but she couldn't laugh. Her tremulous mouth compressed into a bloodless line. Anton had kept their secret to protect his wife. A twenty-one-year-old betrayal had gone to the grave with him. She owed it to her father to keep faith with him. The truth would only cause greater pain and distress and for what gain?

She didn't need whatever Anton had left her. She had her own life to lead and she had no desire to take possession of anything which more rightfully belonged to her father's widow. That would be wrong, morally wrong, she felt. The ring was different. It was her only tangible link to a heritage and a background she had lived all her life without.

'As you can see . . . I'm leaving.' Rosie lifted her bright head high and surveyed the intimidatingly tall, dark Greek with bitter antipathy. 'You have nothing to worry about. I wasn't planning to hang around and embarrass anyone—'

'If it were that simple, we would not be having this distasteful meeting,' Constantine incised fiercely. 'I would be forcibly ejecting you from this house!'

Rosie vented a scornful laugh, her own hot temper steadily rising. 'Really?' she challenged.

He glanced at the open suitcase, his hard mouth twisting. 'You weren't leaving. Possibly you were planning a brief trip somewhere but nothing will convince me that you were about to make a final departure.'

Rosie dealt him a withering glance. 'My, aren't we self-important? What gives you the idea that I would waste my breath trying to convince you of anything?'

A dark surge of blood accentuated the savage slant of his dramatic cheekbones. Naked derision fired his dark eyes. 'I will not lower myself to the level of trading insults with a whore.'

Rosie had a sharp tongue which few attempted to match. She hadn't expected a provocative response. Thwarted fury stormed through her. 'Get out!' she launched at him abruptly. 'Just get out and leave me alone, you ignorant swine!'

'Not before you answer one question,' Constantine asserted in a sudden hiss as he stared broodingly back at her. 'Are you pregnant?'

Rosie stilled in shock, glancing down at the flowing swing blouse she was wearing and then intercepting his narrowed glance travelling in exactly the same direction. Her cheeks crimsoned.

'If you are pregnant . . . then and *only* then could I understand Anton's motivation,' Constantine conceded

grudgingly, and yet he was perceptibly devastated by
what his own imagination had suggested.

And only now had that possibility even occurred to
him, Rosie registered, and boy, did the idea make him
sick! That naturally golden skin had assumed an un-
healthy pallor as presumably the implications of such a
development sank in. This was how Constantine Voulos
would have looked had she revealed her true relationship to Anton, Rosie realised with a sudden stab
of satisfaction.

Few would deny that Anton's child, illegitimate or
otherwise, might have some sort of claim on his estate.
Had she chosen to tell the truth, Constantine would not
have *dared* to insult her. She was Anton's daughter, his
only child, the very last of the Estrada bloodline... and
certainly not some calculating little gold-digger!

'You don't answer me.' Abruptly Constantine swung
away and then he spun just as swiftly back, his strong
features clenched and taut. 'If I have stumbled on the
truth, my opinion of you is unchanged, but I should
apologise for having approached you in such anger.'

Morbid amusement touched Rosie. He was back-
tracking fast on his offensive. Was he afraid of her now,
afraid of the power she might have to disturb the
smoothly planned future he no doubt envisaged for
himself as sole controller of Anton's various business
enterprises? The idea that she might be carrying Anton's
child was a threat that shattered Constantine Voulos.

'But be assured,' he drawled flatly. 'Should there be
a child, every possible test would be required to prove
your claim.'

Rosie was helplessly entertained by the knots he was
tying round himself. Having come up with his own worst-
case scenario, he was forgetting the boundary lines he
had mentioned earlier. 'But wouldn't that be terribly up-
setting for Thespina?'

His breath escaped in a startled hiss, his eyes flashing ferocious gold. 'Your malice is indefensible...'

The instant Rosie had voiced the words she had wished to retrieve them, had realised too late how she would sound. For a moment she had longed to strike back at Thespina and Constantine and now she was bitterly ashamed of that spiteful prompting. She dropped her head, closed the case and tugged it down off the bed. 'I'm not pregnant. Go in peace, Constantine. I am not a threat to either you or Thespina,' she muttered heavily.

Downstairs the doorbell shrilled, breaking the pulsing tension within the bedroom.

'That'll be my cab.' Rosie moved past him with relief. Her knees felt wobbly but she was bolstered by a feeling of innate superiority. Her father had been wrong about Constantine, his ward and son in all but name. Constantine was not, after all, Mr Perfect—well, that was hardly a surprise, was it?

Anton had been naïve to imagine that Constantine would generously open his arms to his own natural child. Rosie had never paid much heed to her father's oft-repeated assurances that if Constantine was ever given the chance he would fall over himself to be welcoming to the sudden advent of a little sister...not that Anton had ever referred to her and Constantine in such gruesome terms as brother and sister!

No, instead Anton had talked with immense warmth and approval about 'family obligations...family support...family honour', blithely ignoring the fact that Rosie would sooner have put an end to her existence than become anyone's obligation! Furthermore she had been born a dyed-in-the-wool cynic.

Constantine had reacted exactly as she had expected to the idea that Anton might have fathered a child— with shock, horror and dismay as he foresaw what an expensive dent such a child might conceivably make in his own financial expectations. Feeling that she was a better person than Constantine Voulos because monetary greed had no hold on her, Rosie held her head high.

'Don't open that door!' Constantine suddenly bit out from behind her.

Rosie's head spun. He was halfway down the stairs, his diamond-bright gaze centred on her with ferocious intensity. 'What the—?'

'Quiet!' he whispered rawly, slashing an overpoweringly arrogant brown hand through the air in emphatic command.

With an exasperation she did not even seek to conceal, Rosie simply ignored his demand and yanked open the front door. Disorientatingly, however, it was not a cab driver who stood on the doorstep. Rosie blinked, gulped and froze.

A small, slim woman in a black suit stared at her in wide-eyed distress, every scrap of colour slowly fading from her olive skin. She took a hesitant step back and then stilled, a look of complete bewilderment drawing her brows together as Constantine's large dark frame appeared behind Rosie.

Faced with her late father's wife in the flesh, Rosie had stopped breathing. Not a muscle moved on her paralysed face as she struggled not to let her horror show. A heavy hand came down on her shoulder like an imprisoning chain of restraint. Constantine said something soft in Greek but Rosie could feel the savage tension holding his big, powerful body in tautly unnatural proximity to hers.

Without warning the older woman lifted her hand and gently caught Rosie's fingers, raising them to study the emerald which trapped the sunlight in its opulent green depths. 'The Estrada betrothal ring,' she whispered unevenly, and then she slowly shook her head in comprehension. 'Of course... Anton gave you the ring for *her!* Constantine, how foolish I have been; I should have guessed ... but why didn't you tell me?'

In receipt of that bemused appeal, Constantine inhaled sharply and Rosie felt his rigidity. 'It did not seem an appropriate time to make an announcement—'

'Only a man could believe that ... as if the news that you are to marry would not bring me joy at *any* time!' Her face wreathed in a delighted smile, all her uncertainty and anxiety vanished, Thespina beamed appreciatively at Rosie. 'Exactly how long have you been engaged to my son?'

'Engaged?' Rosie echoed in a daze of disbelief, the pink tip of her tongue snaking out to moisten her dry lower lip.

'It is very recent,' Constantine drawled flatly.

'But you should have told me,' Thespina scolded in a troubled but tender undertone. 'How could you have believed that I would be distressed by your happiness? If you only knew what madness was in my thoughts as I came to this door—'

A taxi filtered noisily into the driveway. 'My cab,' Rosie muttered in stricken relief.

'You are leaving? But I have only just met you,' the older woman protested in surprise and disappointment.

'I'm afraid that Rosalie has a plane to catch and she's already running late,' Constantine slotted in inventively, closing a lean hand round Rosie's case before she could reach for it again and carrying it swiftly from the house, presumably to enable her to make a faster exit.

'Rosalie ... that is a very ... a very pretty name,' Thespina mused after an odd moment of hesitation, her eyes swiftly veiling before she glanced up again and continued with apparent warmth. 'Forgive me for arriving without an invitation but I shall look forward to spending time with you very soon.'

'I'm sorry I have to rush off like this,' Rosie mumbled in a stifled voice, quite unable to meet the older woman's eyes, twin spots of high colour highlighting her cheekbones.

Constantine already had the door of the cab open. She sensed that if he had had access to supernatural forces a smoking crater would have been all that survived of her presence. But as she began to slide into the cab he caught her with a powerful hand and lowered his arrogant dark head, diamond-hard eyes raking over her with cold menace. 'We have business to discuss. When will you be back?'

'Never.'

'You'll come back for the money all right,' Constantine forecast between gritted teeth, the necessity of keeping his voice down lest he be overheard by Thespina clearly a major challenge to his self-control. 'Now I must force myself to bid you goodbye as a lover would.'

'If you want a knee where it will really hurt, go ahead,' Rosie invited with a venomous little smile and scorching green eyes full of threat.

'*Theos...*' Constantine breathed rawly, his hard fingers biting into her elbow. Bending down with a grim reluctance she could feel, he dropped a fleeting kiss on her brow. One blink and she would have missed it.

Until he touched her, Rosie was as stiff as a little tin soldier, and then she shivered, backed away and scrambled at speed into the cab. It drove off and she could not even make herself look back or wave to add a realistic note to his masquerade. Her heart was racing so fast, she felt physically sick.

Her fingers clenched together tightly on her lap. She felt the ring and she was furious with herself, for hadn't she asked for what she had got and the trouble she had caused? She should have moved out of the house the instant she'd learnt of Anton's death! She should not have openly worn the emerald either.

Her stomach cramped up. She saw Thespina's face as she had first seen it and repressed a shudder. At first Anton's widow had looked devastated. The older woman had somehow found out about the house and she had valiantly come to face whatever or whoever she found there. And, like Constantine, her intelligence had supplied only one possible explanation for Anton's surprising use of a second residence in London...that the husband she had loved and so recently lost had been keeping another woman.

Rosie felt horribly guilty. If Constantine hadn't been the sleek, sneaky type of male who thought fast on his expensively shod feet, what would have happened? If he hadn't pretended that he had given her the Estrada ring because they were engaged, what on earth would Anton's wife have thought?

The sheer intensity of Thespina's relief when she had believed she could lay both house and youthful redhead at Constantine's door rather than at her late husband's had been painful to behold. And her resulting sincere friendship had mortified Rosie. The art of deception was not one of her talents, even if in this case it had been a kindness to protect a woman who had never done anyone the smallest harm and who had already had more than her fair share of disappointment in life.

After all, Thespina had *not* been able to give Anton the child they had both so desperately wanted. One miscarriage after another had dashed their hopes. Only once had Thespina managed to carry a baby to term but the result had been a stillborn son, a shatteringly cruel and final blow to them after so many years of childlessness.

When Thespina had then sunk into deep depression, leaving Anton to struggle alone with his grief, their once strong marriage had begun to crumble. It had been during that period that Anton had been unfaithful with Rosie's mother, Beth... Rosie crushed that discomfiting awareness out. But it was, she discovered, difficult to forget Thespina again. Had they really managed to set the older woman's fears to rest? Had she been convinced?

Before she got on the train that would take her back to Yorkshire, Rosie found herself queuing for a public phone. She dialled the number of the house, praying that Constantine was still there. As soon as she heard his voice, she sucked in a deep breath and said stiffly, 'It's Rosie. Look, I meant what I said earlier. You can keep the money... OK?'

'What sort of a game are you playing?' Constantine launched back wrathfully down the line. 'You think I am impressed by this nonsense? Thespina's gone and we *have* to talk. If she hadn't arrived, I wouldn't have allowed you to leave. I want you back here right now!'

Rosie's teeth ground together. It wasn't as if she had even wanted to speak to Constantine Voulos again and she honestly didn't give two hoots about the money. That had only been her opening salvo, calculated to soothe. Her conscience had driven her to the phone. She felt bad about Thespina. She wanted reassurance that her father's widow hadn't smelled a rat in their performance and had her worst suspicions reawakened. 'I—'

'You think I have got all day to waste on a trashy little tart like you?' Constantine lashed in roaringly offensive contempt.

'Just *who* do you think you are talking to?' Rosie raked back at him, losing her own temper with a speed that left her dizzy. 'Some brain-dead bimbo you can abuse? Well, let me tell you, you overgrown creep, it takes more than a big loud mouth and a flashy suit to impress me and this is one trashy little tart who has no plans *ever* to cross your path again!'

Shaking with temper and mortification, Rosie crashed the phone back down on the cradle and grabbed up her case again, furious that she had put herself out to phone him. Talk about wasting the price of a call! She had got too soft. Anton had done that to her. He had mown down her prickly defences and challenged her to meet his trusting generosity with her own.

But now that her father was gone she could not afford that kind of weakness. This was the *real* world she was back in, not that sentimental, forever sunny place which Anton had cheerfully and somewhat naïvely inhabited. And being soft was only an open invitation to getting kicked in the teeth ...

CHAPTER TWO

MAURICE strolled wearily into the kitchen. Well over six feet in height, he had shoulders like axe handles and a massive chest, but hard physical work had taxed even his impressive resources. His thick mane of long blond hair hung in a limp damp tangle round his rough-hewn features. 'Any chance you bought some beer while you were out shopping?'

Barely lifting her head from the grimy cooker she was scrubbing, Rosie threw him an incredulous glance. 'You've just got to be joking!'

'You can't *still* be mad at me.' Maurice treated her to a look of pained male incomprehension. 'You should have phoned. If I'd had some warning that you were coming back, I'd have brought Lorna in to clean up—'

Scorn flashed in Rosie's eyes. 'Your sister has a full-time job of her own. You should be ashamed of yourself, Maurice. When we moved in here, you promised you'd pull your weight. And the minute my back's turned, what do you do?' she demanded with fiery resentment. 'You turn the cottage into a dirty, messy hovel and my garden into a junkyard!'

Maurice shifted his size thirteen feet uncomfortably. 'I didn't clean up because I wasn't *expecting* you—'

'Stop trying to shift the blame. Put those bulging muscles into shifting those hideous old baths off the lawn and into the barn!'

Maurice grimaced. 'The barn's full.'

23

'Then sell them on and get rid of them! They make this place look like a rubbish tip!'

'Sell them on? Are you nuts? They're worth a packet!' Maurice was openly appalled by the suggestion. 'I make more flogging one bath than you make in a week of selling knick-knacks on your market stall!'

Involuntary amusement filled Rosie, defusing her exasperation. Her conscience stabbed her too. Maurice had been her best friend since she was thirteen. She sighed. 'Look...why don't you go and have a shower? I'll help you clear the garden later.'

But Maurice hovered and cleared his throat. 'I should have said it yesterday but I couldn't find the words... I'm really sorry you lost your dad so soon after him finding you.'

A lump ballooned in Rosie's tight throat. 'He was a nice bloke,' she mumbled, and swallowed hard. 'I was lucky I had the chance to get to know him.'

'Yeah...' A frown darkening his brow, Maurice hesitated before plunging in with two big feet. 'But why leave London in such a rush when he seems to have left you a share of his worldly goods?'

'I *don't* want to talk about that—'

'Rosie...you can't keep on running away from people and situations that upset you.'

A fierce flush lit her cheeks. In self-defence she turned her head away. The reminder that that had been a habit of hers when she was younger was not welcome.

'And you can't leave a legacy hanging in legal limbo either. The executor will be forced to track you down. That's his job.'

'He'll find it difficult. I left no forwarding address.'

'Collect what's coming to you and I bet you could say goodbye to market trading and start up an antique shop here, just the way you always planned,' Maurice pointed out levelly. 'Then between us we could make an offer to buy this place from my uncle instead of renting it.'

Maurice's fatal flaw, Rosie reflected wryly. A complete inability to miss out on any opportunity to make or attract money. And because of it he would probably be a millionaire by the time he was twenty-five. His architectural salvage business was booming.

'You could make a better life for yourself. That's obviously what your father wanted,' Maurice continued with conviction. 'And why do you act so flippin' guilty about his widow? I'm quite sure he hasn't left *her* destitute!'

Rosie spun round, pale and furious, but, having said his piece, Maurice took himself safely upstairs before she even reached the hall. Baulked of the chance to tell him to mind his own business, she scowled on the threshold of the tiny lounge, surveying the all-male debris of abandoned take-aways, squashed beer cans and car magazines. Her nose wrinkled. It was going to take her days to restore the cottage to its former cleanliness. With a rebellious groan, she rubbed at her aching back with a grimy hand and wandered out into the pale spring sunshine.

A silver limousine was in the act of turning in off the road. The impressive vehicle drew to a purring halt behind Maurice's lorry. As Rosie watched with raised brows, a uniformed chauffeur climbed out and opened the rear passenger door. She started to walk towards the barn. It might be the one day of the week that Maurice didn't open for business but he never turned away a customer. However, when a very tall, dark male sheathed in a breathtakingly elegant dove-grey suit emerged from the limo, Rosie stopped dead in her tracks, shock and dismay freezing her fragile features.

Sunlight arrowed over Constantine Voulos's blue-black hair, gilding his tanned skin to gold and accentuating the hard-boned hawk-like masculinity of his superb bone structure. He strode across the yard towards her, his long, powerful legs eating up the distance with a natural grace of movement as eye-catching as that of a lion on the prowl. Rosie connected with glittering dark golden eyes set between dense black lashes. Her stomach clenched, her heart hammering thunderously against her breastbone.

"All women find Constantine irresistible," Anton had told her ruefully. "I don't think he's ever met with a refusal. Unfortunately that has made him rather cynical about your sex."

Rosie surfaced abruptly from that irrelevant memory to find herself being regarded much as she herself might have regarded a cockroach. She flushed, suddenly embarrassingly aware of the soiled sweatshirt and worn jeans she wore and then as quickly infuriated that she should even consider *his* opinion as being of any importance!

'We'll talk inside,' Constantine informed her grimly.

'How the heck did you find me?'

He elevated a sardonic winged ebony brow. 'It wasn't difficult. Anton's desk diary contained this address.'

'Well, I don't want you here,' Rosie retorted with angry heat. 'So you can just take yourself off again!'

'I'm not leaving until we have reached an agreement.' Constantine stared down at her, his arrogant jawline hardening, his nostrils flaring as a black frown built between his brows. 'What age are you?' he demanded abruptly.

'Twenty...not that that's any of your—'

'*Twenty?*' Constantine shot her an appalled look, his sensual mouth twisting with flagrant distaste. '*Christos*...what was Anton thinking of?'

'Not what you're thinking of, anyway!' Rosie scorned.

'But then it takes a male of my experience to understand how the mind of a rapacious little tramp works,' Constantine returned without skipping a beat. 'And you must have put Anton through hell the last weeks of his life!'

Rosie went white with shock. 'What are you talking about?'

Constantine strode past her into the cottage. 'We'll discuss it indoors.'

'I asked you what you were talking about,' Rosie reminded him shakily.

Constantine stood poised on the threshold of the messy, cluttered lounge, his hard-cut profile set in lines of derision. 'You live like a pig!' he breathed in disgust as he swung round again. 'Unwashed...your home filthy. My skin would crawl if I entered that room. You need pest control.'

Stunned into rare silence, Rosie gasped at him as he sidestepped her and swiftly strode back outside again.

'We will stay out here in the fresh air.'

Her cheeks burning with outrage and mortification, Rosie charged out after him again. *'How dare you?'*

'Keep quiet.' Constantine treated her to a chilling look of cold menace. 'Keep quiet and listen well. Anton was one of nature's gentlemen but I'm not and I've already worked out what your game was. I now understand *why* Anton wrote that new will. He drew it up without legal advice, had it witnessed by the servants and then he placed it in his desk the day he returned to London. He was afraid that he would have another heart attack and was seriously worried about your future... and *why* was that?'

Her breath tripped in her throat. 'I—I—'

Icily judgmental dark eyes raked her flustered face. 'Before Anton went on his convalescent cruise, you told him that you were carrying his child... *didn't you?*'

'Don't be ridiculous!' Rosie gasped.

'Your object was to try and force him into divorcing Thespina. You put him under intolerable pressure but you were lying. You weren't pregnant. If you had been, you'd have thrown the news in my face with pleasure yesterday!'

Rosie blinked up at him, her lashes fluttering in bemusement. Even though his suspicions were wildly off beam, she was shattered by the depth of calculation he laid at her door.

Constantine studied her with seething contempt. 'And I'm afraid that Anton chose to deal with a problem that he could not cope with by tipping the whole bloody mess into *my* lap!'

'I don't understand—'

'Of course you don't,' Constantine asserted, his hard mouth curling. 'No doubt you think that he left you a fortune and that all you have to do is sit back and wait for the money to come pouring in. But, sadly for you, your sordid little game-plan backfired . . . Anton did not leave you *anything* in his will!'

Rosie's brow furrowed as she struggled to comprehend what he was telling her. 'But you said—'

'Anton left his estate to me just as he had done in his original will. But in the new version he added a condition to that inheritance. I still inherit . . . but *only* if I marry you!'

'M-marry me?' Her tongue felt too big for her dry mouth and her green eyes were huge with disbelief. '*You* . . . marry . . . *me*?'

'Clearly Anton believed that you *were* pregnant!' Constantine loosed a harsh, embittered laugh as he swung away from her, broad shoulders fiercely taut beneath the fine fabric of his jacket. 'Anton panicked and scribbled out that new will without any reasoned forethought whatsoever. Why did he do that? Because if anything happened to him he wanted his fictional child to be protected and legitimised and he could not face the idea of Thespina finding out the truth.'

'You've got it all wrong,' Rosie protested in a shaken rush. 'My relationship with Anton was strictly platonic. I didn't tell him any lies. I—'

'What sort of a fool do you take me for?' Constantine interrupted with raw contempt. 'You were having an affair. He was living with you in that house and he was besotted with you!'

Her knees giving way, Rosie sank slowly down on the weathered bench at the edge of the overgrown lawn. Even presented with Constantine's twisted interpretation of the facts, she now saw the complete picture and she finally understood. *Anton, how could you do this to me?* she almost screamed, and inside herself she cringed. Unable to freely and publicly acknowledge her as his daughter, her father had nonetheless been determined that her future security should be safeguarded.

And in a moment of madness, in a moment of desperate anxiety about his health, Anton had come up with what only a madman could have seen as a solution! No, not a madman, she immediately adjusted with a suppressed groan, merely an old-fashioned man who honestly believed that all young women were pitifully vulnerable little creatures, helpless without the support and guidance of some big, strong, domineering man.

'It can't be legal...' she whispered tautly.

'It is perfectly legal but it would have been better had that will never seen the light of day,' Constantine acknowledged harshly. 'It *could* be challenged and it might well be overturned in court, because Anton made no provision for what was to happen to his estate in the event of no marriage taking place. As a result his business holdings and accounts are now frozen. But it is impossible to take legal action without exposing Thespina to considerable distress.'

Rosie was finding it very hard to think with clarity. 'Surely she must already know about all this?'

'She does not. Acquainted as she was with the terms of the original will, she has no suspicion of the existence of a later one. It was only discovered when Anton's secretary cleared out his desk two days ago—'

'But what about her? I mean, for heaven's sake, Anton *must* have made some provision for his widow.'

'Thespina is a very wealthy woman in her own right. Anton had no other living relatives. She shared his wish that I should be his heir.' Constantine's shrewd dark gaze skimmed her strained white face and a grim smile clenched his lips. 'And it is not in your own best interests to invite publicity. Open that trashy little mouth and I won't give you a penny!'

Rosie's legs suddenly regained the power of movement. She surged upright, her eyes alight with raw antagonism. 'I don't *want* anything!'

Constantine Voulos studied her with cold, reflective eyes. 'If you think you can drive the price up, you're making a major error of judgement. You will go through a ceremony of marriage . . . and in return you will receive a big, fat cheque and a divorce as soon as I can arrange it.'

'Are you out of your mind?' Rosie demanded incredulously. 'You really think I would go through with a marriage just so that you can get your greedy hands on Anton's estate?'

A sash window above them was noisily opened. 'Rosie? What did you do with all the towels?' Maurice shouted down.

Constantine stiffened and took a step back, the better to get a view of the half-naked young man leaning out of the window. Rosie looked up too, absently conceding that from that angle Maurice looked rather like a blond version of King Kong.

'Sorry...' Maurice muttered, belatedly taking in the male with her and withdrawing his tattooed biceps and extremely hairy chest from view. 'I didn't know you had company—'

'Who the hell is he?' Constantine Voulos raked at Rosie, a rise of dark blood emphasising the savage line of his cheekbones.

'Do you want me to come down and handle this, Rosie?' Maurice enquired.

'When I need you to fight my battles for me, I'll be six feet under!' Rosie bawled back, mortally offended by the offer.

The sash window slid reluctantly down again.

'Anton is scarcely cold in his grave and already you have another man in your bed!' Naked outrage had turned those brilliant black Greek eyes to seething gold.

Rosie's hand flew up and connected with one hard masculine cheekbone with such force that her fingers went numb. Stunned by the blow, Constantine Voulos stared down at her with blatant incredulity.

The thunderous silence chilled her to the marrow.

'I'm sick of you insulting me,' she muttered through chattering teeth, almost as stunned as he was by the violent response he had drawn from her. 'And if you touch me Maurice will pulverise you!'

'He didn't pulverise Anton...did he?'

Even hot with shame at having used Maurice as a threat to hide behind, Rosie registered the oddly roughened quality of Constantine Voulos's deep, dark drawl and the indefinable change in the charged atmosphere.

The tall Greek stared broodingly down at her, smouldering golden eyes alarmingly intent. Involuntarily she met that molten gaze and her heartbeat thundered, her throat closing over, heat igniting in the pit of her stomach. She pressed her thighs together in sudden murderous unease.

'That...that was d-different,' she stammered, utterly powerless in the hold of that entrapping stare which was somehow making her feel things she had never felt before. Sexual things, sexual feelings which filled her not only with astonishment but also with appallingly gauche confusion. Why...how...she didn't understand because she couldn't think straight any more.

Constantine Voulos took a fluid step back, his lean, powerful length emitting an electric tension. Inky black lashes dipped, closing her out again, severing her from the power source that had made every pulse in her treacherous body leap and leaving her disorientated and trembling.

'I haven't got time to play games, Miss Waring. I'll give you twelve hours to think over your position...and then I'll put the pressure on where it hurts most,' Constantine warned in a soft drawl that sent a shiver down her rigid spine. 'With a little help from me, life could become exceedingly difficult. This property is rented. What happens to the junkyard business if the lease isn't renewed?'

Dawning perception filled Rosie's shocked eyes. 'You can't be serious.'

A cold half-smile briefly slanted his hard mouth. 'If I was free to follow my natural inclinations, you'd be begging on the street for your next meal. I'll call again tomorrow morning.'

'How did you know we rented this place?' Rosie prompted helplessly as he walked away from her.

Constantine spun gracefully back. 'And may I put in a special request?' he murmured silkily, ignoring the question. 'You strike me as a woman who knows how to please a man. So have a bath before I show up again.'

Rosie's breasts swelled as she sucked in a heady gush of air. 'Why, *you*—!'

The door of the limousine shut with a soft, expensive clunk. Her head whirling, Rosie stalked into the cottage and threw herself down at the kitchen table. Frustrated fury was hurtling about inside her. For an instant she genuinely thought she might explode. He had actually dared to try and threaten her! But then the stakes he was playing for sounded very high...

What had Anton been worth in terms of cold, hard cash? She shuddered with revulsion. Anton had owned a boatyard, a hotel and a chain of shops in Greece. His business dealings within the UK had been tied up in various speculative property ventures. That nonsensical will! But how very like her father... impulsive and over-protective as he had been.

Her eyes smarted with stinging tears and she gulped. Anton had talked so much about Constantine and always with pride, affection and more than a hint of awe. Wealthy Greek parents expected to have a healthy say in their children's choice of a life partner... he had told her that too.

"Just as well you're Spanish!" she had teased.

"Mallorquin," her father had reproved, still proud as punch of his birth in Majorca even after forty years of living in Greece.

Dear heaven, but she despised Constantine Voulos! Her small hands curled into fists on the table-top. Tramp, whore, trash, tart. And, most unforgivably of all, he had accused her of subjecting Anton to such anxiety that she had shortened his life. Her stomach heaved. Well, he could sling his very worst threats and he would find her immovable. Rosie smiled a little to herself then, her smile slowly growing into a decided smirk. Their landlord *was*, after all, Maurice's uncle. No way was she going through some disgusting charade of marriage just to help

Constantine Voulos circumvent her father's will and profit from it!

'That was the brother from hell...am I right?' Maurice dropped down opposite her and ruefully appraised her hotly flushed face and over-bright eyes. 'Who else do we know rich enough to travel around in a stretch limousine? Not only your dad's substitute son but also large enough and verbal enough to make you so mad you are spitting tacks—'

'Yes, he *was* Anton's favourite, wasn't he? But then I only had four months, not twenty years to make an impression!' Rosie condemned painfully, and then she crammed an unsteady hand against her wobbling mouth, ashamed of the bitter envy she could hear splintering from her words.

'Did you tell him who you were this time?' Maurice enquired gently.

'Why should I? Why should I tell that hateful creep anything? If Anton couldn't trust him with the news, I certainly couldn't!'

Maurice sighed. 'Presumably Voulos came up here to sort out this inheritance of yours.'

A choked laugh was dredged from Rosie. 'I haven't inherited anything! Anton left *me* to Constantine instead!'

Maurice frowned. 'Excuse me?'

'In fact my father tried to *force* me on him...as if I were some brainless little wimp in need of care and protection!' Registering Maurice's still blank scrutiny, Rosie thrust up her chin and the words of explanation came spilling out of her.

'Holy Moses...' Maurice breathed at one stage, but it was his sole interruption. From that point, he listened intently.

'Can you imagine that ignorant, arrogant louse even thinking that I might agree?' Rosie pressed, in a furious appeal for sympathetic accord.

Maurice leant back in his chair, looking very thoughtful. 'Your father has left him in one hell of a fix.'

'I beg your pardon?'

Maurice slowly shook his head. 'Have you any idea how fast a business can go down with its cash flow cut off? No money going in, no money going out—'

'I know next to nothing about Anton's business ventures and I don't much care either,' Rosie said huffily.

'Get your brain into gear, Rosie. Voulos is in a very tight corner. No wonder the guy's furious—'

'Exactly whose side are you on?'

'As always, on the side of common sense and profit,' Maurice told her without apology. 'Do you like the idea of your father's business concerns going bust on a legal technicality? And naturally Voulos doesn't want to drag this whole sorry affair into an open court.'

Rosie reddened uncomfortably, not having considered the situation from either of those angles.

'Voulos came here to bargain with the enemy because he had no other choice. The fastest, easiest solution *is* to meet the terms of your father's will.'

'I can't believe I'm hearing this—'

'And Voulos is offering to compensate you for your time and trouble. I wonder how much he's prepared to put down on the table?' Maurice mused with a slow grin, unaffected by Rosie's look of appalled reproach. 'The trouble with you, Rosie, is that you're an idealist. Voulos isn't and neither am I. You'd cut off your nose to spite your face.'

'Then why don't *you* deal with him when he comes back tomorrow?' Rosie snapped, rising angrily to her feet.

'Do you want me to? I'll willingly stay around and keep an eye on the negotiations. If his temper is anything like yours...well, we don't want bloodshed, do we? What would we do with his body?' Maurice asked cheerfully. 'And dead men can't write big, fat cheques.'

'I won't be here tomorrow,' Rosie informed him thinly.

'Look, it's a business proposition, nothing more. You won't have to live with the guy or like him. And if you won't do it for yourself,' Maurice murmured with a shrewd eye on her frozen face, 'think about your father's employees and what's likely to happen to them if his businesses go down. You can't hit back at Voulos without bringing grief to other people.'

'I don't want to hit back at him, I just want him to *leave me alone*!' Rosie slung in frustrated rage, and stalked out of the room.

Hunched within the capacious depths of an old waxed jacket, Rosie stamped her feet to keep warm and watched her breath steam in the icy air. On a cold, frosty morning the market was always quiet. Maurice strolled up and slotted a plastic cup of coffee into her hand. Rosie surveyed him in surprise. 'What are you doing here?'

Maurice shrugged, carefully avoiding her eyes. 'How's trade going?'

Rosie grimaced. 'It's slow.'

Maurice picked up a large green ceramic rabbit and frowned. 'Isn't this part of your own collection?'

It was Rosie's turn to shrug, faint pink spreading over her cheekbones. 'I'll pick up another one.'

'Nobody's ever going to pay that for it,' Maurice told her, studying the price tag and wincing.

'It's already attracted interest—'

'But not a buyer. You're overpricing it because you can't bear to part with it.'

Frowning at that uncomfortably accurate assistance, Rosie sipped at her coffee. 'Did *he* show up?'

'Yeah...' Maurice rearranged the stock on her stall without raising his head. 'I told him where to find you.'

'You did *what*?' Beneath the brim of her black trilby, Rosie's startled brows shot heavenward.

'I'll watch your stall. Here he comes now...'

As Rosie's horrified eyes fell on Constantine Voulos, her heart turned a somersault and lodged somewhere in the region of her working throat. Her nerveless fingers shook and coffee slopped everywhere without her noticing.

The tall Greek stationed himself on the other side of the stall, his vibrantly handsome features taut with sardonic impatience as he spread a derisive glance around the shabby covered market. 'You do like to play childish games, don't you, Miss Waring?'

Maurice uttered an audible groan. Striding forward, he planted the green rabbit into Constantine Voulos's startled hands. 'Can I interest you in an increasingly rare example of Sylvac pottery?'

'It's a piece of junk,' Constantine gritted, and dumped the item back down at speed.

'You wouldn't know any different, would you?' Rosie snapped as she swept round the stall to check that his rough handling hadn't chipped the rabbit.

Constantine Voulos ignored her to study Maurice with icy contempt. 'I get the picture. You want me to *pay* for the lady's time?'

Maurice folded his arms, his pugnacious aspect belied by the ever-ready sense of humour dancing in his bright blue eyes. 'Suit yourself, mate.'

'What the heck is going on here?' In utter disbelief, Rosie gaped as Constantine flipped out a wallet, withdrew a handful of notes and stuffed them into her pocket. 'I don't want *his* money!'

'When a guy expects to pay for every little thing in life, you ought to satisfy him,' Maurice contended cheerfully. 'Take him across to the pub, Rosie.'

'I'm not going anywhere with him... in fact the two of you can go take a running jump together!' Rosie attempted to move past Constantine but a lean, hard hand snaked out and closed round her forearm. 'Let go of me!'

'You harm a hair of her head and I'll swing for you,' Maurice warned with gentle emphasis as he extended a laden carrier bag. 'Don't forget your purchase, Mr Voulos, and treat it with respect. Rosie's very fond of rabbits—'

In a gesture of supreme contempt, Constantine grasped the bag and dropped it from a height into the metal litter bin opposite. The sound of shattering pottery provoked a stricken gasp from Rosie.

Maurice groaned again. 'There is just no telling some people.'

Wrenching herself violently free of Constantine's hold, Rosie darted over to the bin and looked inside the bag. She paled as she viewed the extent of the damage. It was irreparable. Momentarily her fingertips brushed the broken pieces and then she rounded on Constantine like a spitting tigress, green eyes ablaze. 'How could you do that? How *could* you do that?'

'Why are you shouting?' Incredulous black eyes clashed with hers.

'You selfish, insensitive, snobbish pig...' Rosie condemned wrathfully. 'I was prepared to sell that rabbit, but only if it was going to a good home!'

'Are you unhinged or merely determined to cause a public scene?' Constantine snarled down at her.

'At least I'm not wantonly destructive and spiteful!'

'Spiteful? I wouldn't be caught dead walking around with that ugly piece of tasteless junk!'

With the greatest of difficulty, Rosie haltered her temper. Well, he needn't think he was getting his money back *now*. She swallowed hard, dug her hands into her pockets and walked off. Crossing the pavement, she stepped into the road—or at least she'd started stepping, when a powerful hand closed over her shoulder and yanked her back bodily as a car sped past.

'Do you have a death-wish?' Constantine Voulos grated.

'I'm surprised you didn't push me,' Rosie snapped, shaken by the experience but determined not to betray the fact. 'Oh, I forgot, didn't I? I'm only worth something to you as long as I'm alive and kicking!'

Across the road, she headed in the direction of the small bar used by the market traders, but her companion strode towards the luxury hotel twenty yards further on. Rosie's chin came up. She squared her shoulders and then hesitated. The sooner she dealt with the situation, the sooner he would be gone. A wave of exhaustion swept over her then. She had had little sleep the night before and now she found herself thinking guiltily about her father again.

Anton would have been appalled by the animosity between his daughter and his ward. In drawing up that wretched will, her father had clearly expected her to tell Constantine who she was. Left in ignorance of their true relationship, Constantine had assumed that she was Anton's mistress. What other role could he possibly have assigned to her?

So why hadn't she told him the truth? Rosie's strained mouth compressed. In her mind, Constantine Voulos had been the enemy long before she'd even met him and Anton's death had simply increased her bitterness. She resented the fact that Constantine had grown up secure in *her* father's love and affection. Why not admit it? At the same age she had lost her mother and had been put into the care of the local authorities . . .

Dear heaven, could she really have been that unreasonable? The creeping awareness that she had been unjust and immature filled Rosie with discomfiture.

CHAPTER THREE

Two men in dark suits were waiting in the hotel lobby. They looked tense and sprang forward with a strong suggestion of relief when Constantine appeared. A spate of low-pitched Greek was exchanged. Striding ahead of them into the quiet, almost empty lounge bar, the younger man rushed to pull out a pair of comfortable armchairs beside the log fire.

Fluidly discarding his black cashmere overcoat, Constantine sank indolently down and snapped imperious fingers. While Rosie looked on in fascination, the second man stationed behind him inclined his head to receive instructions. The waitress was summoned and drinks were served at spectacular speed.

'What's with Laurel and Hardy?' Rosie nodded in the direction of the two men.

'Dmitri and Taki are my security men.'

'I won't ask why you need them. Your personality kind of speaks for itself.' Bodyguards, for goodness' sake? To conceal her embarrassment, Rosie whipped off her hat and a mass of wildly colourful spiralling curls cascaded round her shoulders. In a gesture of impatience, she finger-combed her hair back off her face. As she removed her jacket to reveal the ancient guernsey sweater she wore beneath, she intercepted a disturbingly intent stare from her companion.

'What are you looking at?' she demanded aggressively.

An aristocratic ebony brow climbed but rich dark eyes gleamed with grudging amusement and without warning a devastating smile slashed his hard features. That smile

41

blinded Rosie like a floodlight turned on in the dark.
Taken by surprise, she squirmed like a truculent puppy
unsure of its ground. Her eyes colliding with that night-
dark gaze, she experienced the most terrifying lurch of
excitement. Her stomach muscles clenched as if she had
gone down in a lift too fast.

'Your hair is a very eye-catching colour,' he murmured wryly.

'And usually only rag-dolls have corkscrew curls,'
Rosie completed in driven discomfiture, carefully
studying the soft drink she had snatched up, her palms
damply clutching the glass and her hands far from steady.

In the church she had assumed that it was the shock
of meeting him which had shaken her up. But yesterday
she had experienced a magnetic and undeniably sexual
response that had briefly, mortifyingly reduced her to a
positive jelly of juvenile confusion. But it wasn't her
fault—no, it definitely wasn't—and there wasn't anything personal about it either, she told herself bracingly.
So there was no need for her to be sitting here with her
knees locked guiltily together and her cheeks as hot as
a furnace.

It was *his* fault that she was uncomfortable. He was
staggeringly beautiful to look at, but then that wasn't
the true source of the problem. Constantine Voulos had
something a whole lot more dangerous. A potent, sexually devastating allure that burned with electrifying
heat. Out of the corner of her eye, Rosie watched an
older woman across the lounge feasting her attention on
Constantine's hard-cut, hawk-like profile and felt
thoroughly vindicated in her self-examination.

'Let us concede that we met for the first time in in-
auspicious circumstances,' Constantine murmured. 'But
the time for argument is now past. There is no reason
why this unfortunate affair should not be settled quietly
and discreetly.'

Rosie sat forward, tense as a drawn bowstring. 'I haven't been honest with you,' she began stiffly. 'I made things worse than they needed to be but then you didn't make things easy either... leaping off on a tangent, making wild assumptions and insulting me—'

'I don't follow.' Impatience edged the interruption.

Pale and tense, Rosie snatched in a ragged breath. 'I'm not who you think I am. I wasn't Anton's mistress...' She coloured as she said that out loud. 'I'm his daughter, born on the wrong side of the blanket... or whatever you want to call it...'

Constantine Voulos dealt her an arrested look and then his gaze flared with raw incredulity. 'What the hell do you hope to achieve by making so grotesque a claim?'

Rosie's brows drew together. 'But it's true... I mean, I suppose you have every reason not to want to believe me, but Anton *was* my father.'

His mouth curled with distaste and impatience. 'You really are a terrible liar. Had Anton been related to you in *any* way, his lawyers would have been well aware of the fact.'

Rosie stared blankly back at him. It had never occurred to her that the truth might be greeted with outright contempt and instant dismissal. 'But he didn't tell anyone—'

'And the proof of this fantastic allegation?'

'Look, it was Anton who traced *me*—'

'Let me relieve your fertile imagination of the belief that the nature of your relationship with Anton has any bearing on the size of the cheque I will write,' Constantine broke in with withering bite. 'And now please stop wasting my time with ridiculous fairy stories!'

Rosie dropped her head, a surge of distress making her stomach churn. Proof? She had *never* had any proof! Anton's name was not on her birth certificate and Constantine was so full of himself, so convinced that she was an inveterate liar, that he wouldn't even listen to her. For the first time she realised that with Anton's death she had been dispossessed of any means of proving that he had been her father. And even though she had never planned to do anything with that knowledge that reality had a terrible, painful finality for her.

'Let's get down to business,' Constantine suggested drily.

Utterly humiliated by his disbelief, Rosie wanted very badly to simply get up and walk out. Only the grim awareness that he would follow her and fierce pride kept her seated.

'With your agreement, arrangements will be made for the marriage ceremony to take place as soon as possible. The legal firm I use in London will liaise with you. When this matter has been dealt with, you will be most generously compensated,' Constantine assured her smoothly before going on to mention a sum which contained a breathtaking string of noughts. 'All I ask from you is discretion and also the return of the Estrada betrothal ring.'

Rosie looked up, her face drawn and empty of animation. 'No.'

'It is a family heirloom. It must be returned.'

'No,' Rosie said again.

'In spite of its age, the ring has no great financial worth. The stone is flawed.'

Rosie flinched, nausea lying like a leaden weight in her over-sensitive stomach. 'There must be some other way that the will could be sorted out.'

'If there was, do you seriously think that I would be here demanding that you secretly go through such a ceremony with me?'

The harsh, derisive edge to the question made Rosie flush. No, Constantine Voulos had no other choice. His very presence here told her that. Nor could she fail to see how deeply and bitterly he resented the necessity of being forced to ask for *her* co-operation.

'But Thespina seemed to like me,' she began awkwardly. 'And she already thinks we're engaged. Is there any need for all this secrecy?'

'If she knew who you really were, do you think she would like you?' Constantine breathed scathingly. 'She'd be furious. As for the engagement . . . I'll tell her it was a soon regretted impulse on my part. There is no need for her to know about the marriage. I don't want you meeting her again.'

Rosie's eyes fell uneasily from his. She might not have been Anton's mistress but even as his daughter she would be no more welcome an advent in Thespina's life. And if she agreed to a secret marriage of convenience Constantine would inherit and Anton's business interests *and* presumably his employees would continue to prosper. Thespina would have no reason to become suspicious again . . . indeed, everything would go back to normal, just as if Rosie herself had never existed.

Rosie lifted her head, green eyes veiled. 'You keep your money, I keep the ring.' Pulling on her jacket, she stood up. 'Now if you don't mind I'd like to leave.'

'I prefer to pay for favours. Have I your agreement?'

'I'm agreeing only out of respect for Anton's memory...just you understand that. But how could you understand it? You only think in terms of financial gain,' she completed in disgust, and spun on her heel.

'I think only in terms of the well-being of Anton's *wife*,' Constantine countered with icy emphasis.

Contempt froze her fragile features as she turned back to him. 'That sounds so impressive coming from a male who sleeps with another man's wife whenever the fancy takes him!'

Taken by surprise, Constantine Voulos sprang upright. '*Christos . . .*'

Rosie widened her huge green eyes, revitalised by the shock stiffening his darkly handsome features. 'Your long-running secret affair with the actress, Cinzia Borzone. So don't go all pious on me!'

As Rosie walked away, head held high, she heard the ground-out surge of explosive Greek that followed that revelation. The depth of her knowledge about his private life had come as a most unwelcome surprise to Constantine Voulos.

Certainly Anton had lamented long and hard on the topic of that unsuitable relationship. In *his* opinion, Constantine had, at the tender age of twenty-five, fallen live into the paws of a designing married woman with a husband who was perfectly content to turn a blind eye to his wife's infidelity if the financial rewards were great enough.

And although several times over the past four years Anton and Thespina had been encouraged to hope that the affair had run its course Cinzia had ultimately appeared to triumph over every other woman who entered Constantine's life. Maybe that situation had even been on Anton's mind when he'd changed his will, Rosie reflected ruefully.

Anton had had the optimistic hope that marriage would cure Constantine's desire for another man's wife. And long before his death Rosie had known that her father cherished a happy daydream in which *she* and Constantine met, fell madly in love and married, thereby bringing his daughter into the family by the only possible route that would not hurt his wife.

Maurice frowned in surprise when she rejoined him. 'Don't tell me you walked out on Voulos again.'

'No. I agreed . . . OK? I even told him who I was this time.' Rosie gave her friend a grim little smile. 'Only he didn't believe me.'

Taken aback, Maurice stared at her. 'Why not?'

'Why should he have? I don't even look like Anton. I don't have any evidence of who I am either. In fact, sitting there with Constantine Voulos, those four months started feeling like a rather embarrassing juvenile fantasy,' Rosie confided thinly, tucking herself back behind her stall. 'So, if you don't mind, I'd rather not discuss it any more—'

'But Anton had all those photos your mother sent him and he must have had other things.'

'If he did he never mentioned them and heaven knows what he did with those photos.' Tired and drained of emotion, Rosie shrugged. 'It doesn't matter much now, does it?'

Late that night, the front door slammed noisily. Half-asleep on the sofa after an evening of exhaustive cleaning, Rosie sat up with a start. Maurice burst into the lounge looking excited and tossed a glossy but somewhat dog-eared magazine down on her lap. 'Lorna had this. She was able to tell me all about Constantine Voulos.'

'What are you talking about?' Rosie mumbled drowsily.

'My sister has a stack of magazines about the rich and famous. The minute I mentioned his name it rang a bell with her and she looked that out for me. Voulos is a genuine Greek tycoon,' Maurice informed her impressively. 'He's loaded! The guy was *born* into a fortune. Your father was only a small-time businessman in comparison.'

'So?' Rosie groaned as she stood up.

'Rosie…you don't want to sign anything away before or after that wedding,' Maurice warned her. 'Voulos doesn't need your father's estate. He's already rich as sin. It's all wrong that you should be cut out just because the guy doesn't want you around!'

'I'm going to bed—'

'I'm trying to look out for you, Rosie. *You* have got rights too,' Maurice told her with stark impatience. 'Your dad would turn in his grave if he knew what Voulos was doing!'

'Maurice, Constantine Voulos has not one thing that I want.'

But was it true that Constantine was wealthier than her father had ever been? Anton certainly hadn't travelled around in a chauffeur-driven limo or hauled bodyguards in his wake. She shrugged. Either way, what did it matter to her? And even if Constantine was filthy rich it didn't mean he couldn't also be disgustingly greedy.

But she still took that magazine to bed with her. There was a picture of Constantine, looking spectacularly dark and smooth and dangerous in a dinner jacket. A beautiful blonde was clutching his arm as if she was afraid he was about to escape. Rosie surveyed the blonde with pity. Constantine was the sort of male animal you kicked hard and walked away from. He would thrive on that kind of brutal treatment and come back for more. Even *she*, with her limited experience of the male sex, had worked that out at first glance.

As Rosie drove herself to the chosen register office in a nearby town three weeks later, she was struggling to suppress a deep sense of unease. Even if she couldn't condone her father's ill-considered attempt to endow her with the lifestyle she might have had as his legitimate daughter, she knew that he had written that will in sincerity and that made her feel guilty and disloyal.

As she drew her little van to a reluctant halt in the car park, she espied the now familiar limousine and pulled a face. Constantine's bodyguards were outside the register office, on the lookout for her. Neither was dressed for the chill of a late Yorkshire spring. They were blue with cold and the younger man, Taki, was sneezing. Both men fell over themselves in their eagerness to open the door for her and follow her indoors.

'You're late,' Constantine grated, striding forward to intercept her.

'But I'm here,' Rosie pointed out flatly. 'Don't look a gift-horse in the mouth.'

Incredulous dark eyes roved over her waxed jacket and jeans. '*Theos*...didn't Anton buy you any decent clothes?'

Rosie reddened, her mouth tightening as she took in the full effect of his exquisitely cut navy pinstripe suit, white silk shirt and gold tie. 'Surely you didn't think I would get all dolled up for this charade?'

'This is not a charade,' Constantine growled in a repressive undertone. 'We are about to undergo a legal and binding ceremony.'

A split second after a clerk approached them to invite them into the room where the civil marriage service would take place. Rosie froze. 'I don't like this at all,' she whispered frantically. 'I wish I hadn't agreed—'

Impatient long brown fingers enclosed her own and urged her onward. 'You will go through with it for Thespina's sake.'

Rosie paled at that cruel reminder of her father's vulnerable widow. This was a cover-up, she reminded herself, an unpleasant but essential manoeuvre to enable Constantine to inherit Anton's estate without challenging his will. She focused on a rather tired flower arrangement on a nearby table and then minutes later, from somewhere outside herself, she watched in helpless amazement as Constantine lifted her ice-cold hand and slotted a slender gold ring onto her wedding finger.

'I believe you drove yourself here,' Constantine murmured on the pavement outside. 'Give me your car keys.'

Rosie frowned. 'My car keys?' She already had them in her hand. 'Why?'

Without hesitation, Constantine swiped her keyring from between her fingers, tossed it deftly to Taki and said something in Greek.

It happened so fast that Rosie blinked in bemusement as Taki sped off with her keys. 'What on earth do you think you're playing at?' she demanded furiously.

'He will drive your vehicle home. We're spending the night at a hotel.' Constantine closed a restraining hand round her shoulder as his limousine pulled in by the kerb.

'*We* ... Say that again?' Rosie shot aghast eyes to his dark, strong face.

'Were we to part immediately after the ceremony, it would look very suspicious.'

'To whom?' Rosie gasped.

'Should this arrangement of ours ever be questioned, I will not lay myself open to a charge of having entered the marriage on false pretences—'

'But that's exactly what you've done!'

'And wouldn't it be very foolish of me to make that obvious?'

'No way am I spending the night with you!' Rosie told him hotly.

'You have no choice. This is part of the deal.'

Rosie folded her arms and stood her ground. 'No way,' she said again. 'I wouldn't trust you as far as the foot of the street!'

'Do you require assistance to get into the car?' Dangerous dark eyes of warning rested on her.

For an instant, Rosie hesitated, and then she climbed into the limousine in one quick, angry movement. 'A man who has to threaten to use brute strength to get his own way is a pathetic apology for a man!'

'Pity me, then,' Constantine advised with silken unconcern, treating her to a long, lingering scrutiny that made her shift and tauten. 'Every time you shout at me I want to slap you down so hard you'll be scared to raise your head again. I can't say that you bring out the best in me and you must have put on one hell of an act for Anton. Anton would have run a mile from that mouth of yours.'

'There's nothing wrong with my mouth—'

'It's an incredibly sexy mouth...until you open it.' Night-dark eyes partially veiled by lush black lashes rested on the full pink lips in question.

Sharply disconcerted, Rosie flushed. 'Don't talk to me like that.'

'Don't tell me what I can and can't say,' Constantine drawled softly. 'Nobody does that.'

Involuntarily, Rosie stiffened, feeling that sudden chill even in the warmth of the luxurious car. 'I'm not prepared to stay at a hotel with you.'

'But you will. It's part of our little arrangement. I will not run the risk that at some future date this marriage could be set aside as null and void. I am merely ensuring that we abide by the law to the letter.'

Silence fell, thick with tension, between them.

'Just how much *did* Anton tell you about me?' Constantine demanded abruptly.

'Much more than I wanted to hear, believe me!'

His sensual mouth hardened and twisted. 'We were close but evidently not close enough,' he mused grimly. 'He was too ashamed to tell me about you—'

'Anton was *not* ashamed of me.'

'Anton was a very happily married man until you came along.'

Rosie bit her lip and made no response. Anton had spent several years and a lot of money striving to trace his illegitimate daughter. For the first nine years of her life he had received photographs of her on every birthday, but her mother, Beth, had included no return address.

Rosie had often wondered why her mother had taken the trouble to secretly post those photos to Anton's London office. Had the exercise simply been an annual embittered reminder of the brief affair which had messed up Beth's life and cost Anton his only child?

Rosie didn't know. By the time she had heard the full story of her parentage, her mother had been dead for many years. But she could still remember her mother struggling to handle the brooding bitterness of a husband who had never been able to forgive her for marrying him when she was pregnant by another man. Beth had been dead only a week when Rosie's stepfather had called in the social services to tell them loudly and aggressively that he had no intention of keeping a child who wasn't his. That had been *his* revenge.

The limousine drew up in front of a country-house hotel. Rosie climbed out and hovered. 'This is ridiculous.'

'It wouldn't look quite so ridiculous if you weren't dressed like some revolting teeny-bopper hitchhiker I happened to pick up on the road here!'

In the intimidatingly elegant foyer and from a distance of almost twenty feet Rosie watched him sign the register. The hotel receptionist was far too well trained to stare but she squinted surreptitiously at Rosie. Rosie went pink and turned her back.

On the first floor, they were shown into a beautifully furnished suite. Seeing the connecting door, Rosie hastened through it to explore. Beyond lay only one bedroom complete with bathroom. He was out of his mind, she thought incredulously.

'If you think I am spending the night in there with you, you are living in a world of fantasy!'

Constantine dealt her a sardonic glance. 'I take the bedroom. You get the couch.'

Momentarily, Rosie couldn't get oxygen into her lungs. Wild-eyed, she stared back at him.

'I'll ruffle the pillows in the morning. Taki also has instructions to collect a change of clothes for you. No doubt Maurice will rise nobly to the occasion,' Constantine continued with smooth derision. 'I think your muscle-bound boyfriend would sell you to cannibals for the right price.'

'Maurice is a friend, not a lover!'

Constantine elevated an unimpressed brow, his expressive mouth curling.

'You have *such* a dirty mind,' Rosie told him fiercely.

Unexpectedly the beginnings of a smile tugged at the corners of his ruthless mouth. Brilliant black eyes rested intently on her furious face. 'So much fire and spirit. That intrigues me. If you hadn't been Anton's woman first, I would be very tempted to take you to my bed.'

Rosie went from fury into deep shock. Her lips moved but no sound came out.

'And I guarantee that within five minutes you would be eating out of my hand like a tame dove trained to please,' Constantine forecast with a feral flash of even white teeth.

Rosie unglued her tongue from the roof of her mouth. She was trembling. 'You have an incredible imagination!'

Constantine spread his elegant brown hands in a gesture of flagrant mockery. 'But how can you try to deny what we both know to be true? The very first time you saw me, you felt the heat rise between us. I felt it too. Raw sexual attraction, nothing more complex—'

Rosie forced a jagged laugh that hurt her throat. 'Your conceit is unbelievable.'

'Never challenge a Greek unless you're prepared to meet fire with fire,' Constantine drawled softly. 'But then perhaps that is exactly what you would like...?'

The atmosphere was so tense that her heartbeat thundered while those black eyes smouldered over her in challenging gold enquiry. A brisk knock sounded on the door and she jumped. Dmitri entered.

On dreadfully wobbly legs, Rosie retreated to the couch. There were goose-bumps all over her skin and she was horribly aware of the dull ache in her breasts and the painful tightness of her nipples. Just by standing there, just by looking at her like that, talking to her like that, *he* had done that to her body. That was scary; that was very scary indeed.

He had attacked on her weakest flank, smiling at her animosity because he could afford to smile while he laid bare the sexual charge between them. 'Raw sexual attraction'—no, that didn't embarrass him. Why should it? Constantine was Greek to the backbone, earthy in his blunt acknowledgement of nature's most driving force. But perhaps Rosie was most shaken by his unashamed admission that what she was feeling *he* was feeling too...

But then he was ninety per cent sexual predator, only ten per cent civilised. Hadn't she got great taste? Bitterly resenting the unfamiliar sense of inadequacy assailing her, Rosie watched Dmitri flip out a sleek portable computer and set it on the desk by the window. A porter entered with a fax machine and hurried to install it. Then a waiter arrived with a tray of coffee...coffee for *one*! Rosie's eyes flared. Seeking guidance, the waiter tried to catch her attention but Rosie ignored him, too proud to indicate a need for anything that would be supplied as a mere afterthought.

Meanwhile Constantine talked in fluent French on a mobile phone, his back turned to her, one large brown hand dug into the pocket of his well-cut, elegant trousers, his silk-lined jacket elbowed back to display a murderously flat stomach, the jut of a lean, taut masculine hip and long, long, powerful thighs. He looked so incredibly good *in* his clothes, she stopped breathing altogether at the thought of what he must look like *out* of them. Then, truly appalled by a kind of curiosity she had never experienced before, Rosie reddened fiercely, lifted the remote control within her reach and switched the television on to a satellite music channel.

'If you want to listen to music, use the set in the bedroom,' Constantine told her, breaking off from his call with a look of extreme irritation and then swinging away again.

Rosie bounced upright, digging angry hands into her pockets. 'I'll go out for a walk.'

His imperious dark head turned. 'No. You stay in the suite. Go and wash your hair or something,' he advised impatiently. 'I have work to do.'

Rosie breathed in so deeply, she was frightened she would burst and scream round the ceiling like a punctured balloon. 'I do what *I* like, Mr Voulos.'

'Not around me, you don't.' Casting aside the mobile phone, Constantine slung her a long, hard look of warning.

Her hands balled into fists inside her pockets. 'And what makes you think that?'

'I should have locked you in the boot of the limo for the night and hired someone else to play the bridal role. What am I getting in return for my money? You look about fifteen in that get-up. The hotel staff must think I'm a pervert...not that anyone in their right mind would credit that we *are* a newly married couple! And when you're not sulking it's yap, yap, yap.' Flashing black eyes raked over her in unconcealed exasperation. 'It's like having a chihuahua, snapping and snarling at my heels!'

Rosie shuddered with incredulous wrath. 'How *dare* you?'

'If you had had *me* in your bed for four months, you would at least know when to shut up and make yourself scarce!'

'You would be dead,' Rosie spelt out in a voice that shook with pure rage.

'You think so?' A slow-burning smile of savage amusement slashed his strong dark features. 'No, I think you would have learnt how to behave around me by the end of the first week. Unlike Anton, I'm low on patience and high on expectation and right now you are scoring zero all the way down the line.'

'Not ten minutes ago you were trying to make a pass at me!' Rosie condemned in outrage. 'But you knew you weren't going to get anywhere, so now you're being deliberately offensive!'

Constantine tilted his arrogant dark head to one side and narrowed his eyes to allow them to wander with slow incredulity over her. '*That* was a *pass*?' he derided in disbelief. 'So that's what's biting you. I'm supposed to be panting with uncontrollable lust, am I? And you call *me* conceited? At this moment you have all the sex appeal of a vagrant—'

'If you say one more word, I'll . . . I'll . . .'

A winged ebony brow rose enquiringly. 'You'll what? You'll *bite*?'

Speechless with rage, Rosie could only gasp, green eyes blazing like emeralds in her hotly flushed face.

Constantine dealt her a cold smile of menacing strength. 'Let's get one thing straight, little rag-doll. You bite me, you'll get bitten back to the bone. And if you're cherishing the wild and ambitious hope that I plan to become your next wealthy meal-ticket you're losing touch with reality. I felt the heat but I have no intention of melting—'

'You ignorant, arrogant swine!' Rosie splintered, finding her tongue.

'I have this curious feeling that our minds are finally meeting in perfect harmony,' Constantine murmured lazily, his lush black lashes lowered over brilliant dark, incisive eyes. 'And the thought for the day is... better to be an old man's darling than a young man's fool!'

Rosie shivered with rage and backed away from him. Never in her life had she felt as if she could kill... until *now*. She wanted Maurice's muscles. She wanted to knock Constantine off his feet, swing him around her head and then pound him into a pulp.

The mobile phone buzzed again.

Rosie reached the bedroom door on wobbling legs.

'Can you type?' Constantine enquired without warning and it was as if the previous conversation had not taken place.

'T-type?' Rosie stammered helplessly.

'Take dictation?' he prompted impatiently. 'The fewer people who are in on this arrangement the better... but it's bloody inconvenient not to have my personal staff around.'

'I don't type or take dictation,' Rosie breathed through rigidly compressed lips.

Constantine angled a scathing, unsurprised glance over her slight, stiff-as-a-board figure. 'But I bet you'd be a rousing success at climbing cutely onto any middle-aged employer's lap.'

CHAPTER FOUR

AN HOUR later, Taki having delivered an embarrassingly unimpressive plastic carrier bag to the bedroom, Rosie turned from her incredulous examination of what Maurice had packed on her behalf and reached immediately for the phone.

'Are the contents of this bag supposed to be a joke, Maurice?' Rosie demanded, threading outraged fingers through the diaphanous nightdress, the silky little raspberry-coloured slip dress and sheer tights. Three-inch-heeled strappy velvet shoes and the box of make-up that had been a Christmas gift from his sister completed the collection of impractical items. Naturally there was neither a change of underwear nor a toothbrush included.

'It's your wedding night. I thought you might want to dress up.'

'Ha, ha,' Rosie gritted, unamused.

'Has Voulos asked you to sign anything yet?' Maurice prompted worriedly.

'Not even the hotel register.'

'I think he knew a pre-nuptial contract mightn't be worth the paper it was written on if it ever came before a British court but he's sure to try and get you to sign something surrendering any financial claim on him. On the other hand,' Maurice mused, 'should the Press get to hear about the marriage, his goose would be fairly cooked.'

'Maurice, I'm very fond of you but right at this minute I am thoroughly ashamed of your greed!' Rosie spelt out angrily, and slammed down the receiver.

She called Room Service and a menu was delivered. She wasn't very hungry but she put in as much time as possible working her way through a pot of tea and a plate of chicken sandwiches. As a rule she never watched much television and she paced the floor in growing boredom and resentment, an unappreciative audience to the buzz of the fax and the stream of constant phone calls in the next room.

By seven, she was ready to go stir-crazy and wondering why she was allowing *him* to intimidate her into remaining hidden in the suite. What did it matter if anyone saw her downstairs alone? They would hardly be surprised. Her pretend bridegroom was patently a selfish, insensitive workaholic.

An utterly hateful, bad-tempered swine too, Rosie reflected fierily as she freshened up in the bathroom and reached for the sheer tights. The heart-stopping looks of a dark angel crossed with the temperament of a snarling beast. So brutally sarcastic as well. He never missed a chance to put her down.

Lack of physical size had always meant that Rosie's tongue was her first line of defence. She was furiously conscious that for a few minutes in that room next door Constantine had overpowered her with the smooth, ricocheting speed and force of his derisive attacks. She hadn't made a single dent in that tough hide of his! No, she had gone into retreat. And yet here she was, doing him a huge favour for free, and what thanks was she getting for it?

Well, tomorrow morning, when she tore up his precious cheque in front of him, she would be the party holding the moral high ground then, wouldn't she? Rosie tilted her chin as she added a little colour to her lips and experimented with a touch of shadow on her eyelids. When she opened the door a crack, Constantine was talking in cold, quelling tones on the phone.

'Tomorrow isn't good enough,' he was saying with icy precision. 'When I say move, I expect a sprint, not a soft-shoe shuffle.'

Rosie peeped out, saw him poised with his back to the room, tiptoed along the wall and crept out as quietly as a mouse. In the corridor, she ignored his hovering security men and calmly slipped on her shoes while inwardly wincing at the sound of Taki's harsh cough. However, when she stepped into the lift, the young security man stepped in behind her. And when she strolled into the low-lit, intimate bar on the ground floor he was still tailing her.

Well, at least his presence would save her from the boredom of having to pretend to read the glossy hotel brochure she had brought down with her, she reflected ruefully. She had planned to look occupied lest some cruising predatory male see her solitary state as some kind of invitation.

Every male head in the bar turned to follow her elegant passage. Titian curls rioted round the perfect oval of her face. Shoestring straps curved over smooth white shoulders, the raspberry silk flowing fluidly against slender curves, the hem caressing surprisingly long and shapely legs. Rosie selected a seat. Taki hailed a waiter and then went off into another choking bout of coughing.

'You should be in bed.' Rosie flicked the young Greek a look of grudging sympathy as she noted the feverish flush on his cheekbones. 'But I bet you'd have to go into convulsions and drop dead before Constantine would notice.'

Shivering, he frowned, his grasp of English clearly of the basic variety, and then he started coughing again and spluttering what sounded like a croaking apology. Rosie groaned, 'Oh, for goodness sake, sit down! You need a hot whisky with cloves in it. That should clear your head and help you to sleep.'

He slumped hesitantly down on a chair, regarding her with bashful, bemused eyes. Rosie ordered a double for him and urged him to drink it all down. He shook his curly dark head uncertainly.

'Drink it!' Rosie commanded with force.

He was much more obedient than Constantine. Indeed after that one drink Taki became astonishingly garrulous, but since he was talking in his own language Rosie couldn't understand a word. She suspected that might be just as well. A look of intense admiration now glowed in the young Greek's befuddled stare.

'What the hell do you think you're playing at?' The seething demand penetrated Rosie's introspection at the same time as a big black shadow fell over the table. Her bright head lifted, her hand jerked and wine slopped out of her glass.

Taki shot upright and fell noisily over a chair. Taking in the situation at a glance, Dmitri surged forward to lift and steady the younger man and urge him towards the exit. His superb bone structure a mask of outrage, Constantine stared at Rosie, his eyes molten gold and as hard as diamonds.

'I had no idea you'd left the suite. You will return there immediately,' he ordered in a low-pitched growl of raw intimidation.

There was something about Constantine, something about that outrageous domineering attitude, that brought out the very worst in Rosie even when that same attitude could send an undeniable current of fear shooting through her veins. 'Or what? I get forty lashes before midnight? I'm just sitting here having a quiet drink—'

'Upstairs,' Constantine bit out, pale with rage beneath his olive skin.

'You Tarzan, me Jane?' Rosie fed the flames with a flashing little smile of warning. 'I don't think so.'

'We have an agreement,' Constantine thundered in a repressive undertone that shimmied down her taut spine like abrasive sand on silk. 'And you are behaving in an inappropriate manner.'

Rosie tilted her head back, her fiery tresses gleaming as bright as her eyes. 'Frankly, I think I'm behaving very much in character. I'm playing a bimbo,' she told him helpfully. 'Lots of bimbos marry rich older guys who bore the pants off them—'

'Say that again,' Constantine invited, a slow rise of dark colour accentuating the taut slant of his high cheekbones.

'So the neglected little wife gets restless and comes down to the bar to watch life pass her by,' Rosie continued with a sad, soulful aspect.

'People are looking at us.' His expressive mouth hard as iron, eyes blazing, Constantine sank down with controlled animal grace into a seat. But he still reminded her of a ferocious tiger prevented at the very last moment from springing.

'Of course they are...and congratulations—you're adding real veracity to this masquerade. Enter suspicious bridegroom in a seething temper. I shall try to look sufficiently quelled by the display,' Rosie promised, hanging her head and shrinking her shoulders as if she were withstanding the blast of his righteous wrath with suitable humility. 'But I am certainly not going back upstairs to vegetate in that bedroom.'

Constantine breathed in very, very slowly and deeply in the rushing silence.

Rosie grinned. 'You're shrewd, Constantine, I'll give you that. You see, if you tried trailing me out of here by force, someone might feel they had to intervene on my behalf.'

'Tomorrow morning cannot come soon enough for me,' Constantine swore with a feral flash of gritted white teeth.

'I know . . . we're not exactly a match made in heaven.'

'You are very brave in public places.'

'You're a very big guy.'

'So is Maurice.'

Rosie smiled. 'Maurice is as gentle as a lamb. He *never* loses his temper.'

'But then you wear the pants in that relationship,' Constantine interposed with scathing bite, a look of blatant disgust in his gaze.

'I expect you like women servile and adoring. You were born out of time, Constantine. You should have been an Arab potentate with a harem. Do you know that concubines were trained to crawl across the floor of their master's bedroom and up under the covers from the foot of the bed?' Rosie told him informatively.

Luxuriant black lashes dipped. His sensual mouth twisted. 'I am in the middle of a takeover bid for a company I have been working to acquire for some months.' The lashes shot up to reveal savagely impatient dark eyes. 'I don't trust you. I am not leaving you down here alone to pick up some man on what is supposed to be our wedding night.'

'I am not going to pick up a man. I have *never* picked up a man in my life.'

'I saw how those men at the bar were watching you. Like drooling, sex-starved sailors on shore leave!' Constantine grated, a faint flush highlighting his taut cheekbones. 'You wouldn't need to flex a fingernail. No decent woman would sit in a bar on her own—'

'I had Taki in tow.'

'You got him blind drunk!'

'He's got a bad cold and he was feeling foul and he must have a very low tolerance level for alcohol.' Rosie grimaced. 'But I told him to have a drink—'

'And his miscalculation in doing so will cost him his employment.'

Rosie went white with shock. 'That's not fair, Constantine. I *insisted* that he had that drink—'

'Did you also insist that he made love to you?'

'What the heck are you trying to imply?'

Black eyes glittered, his nostrils flaring. 'I heard what he was saying to you . . . a member of my staff making romantic advances to my wife—'

'Your wife? I am *not* your wife!' Rosie cut in with incredulous heat and vigour. 'I wouldn't be your wife for a million pounds!'

'Oh, I think you could push yourself for that amount . . . indeed a great deal less,' Constantine asserted with raw, biting cynicism. 'What price did you put on your body for Anton? He stuck you in a rented house. He didn't even buy you the roof over your head—' As the remainder of the wine in her glass splashed his strong, dark face, he broke off and stared at her with charged, thunderous disbelief.

Rosie stood and returned that look with venomous loathing. 'You make Neanderthal man look like Einstein!'

Constantine made it into the lift before she could get the doors closed on him. Consumed by rage, Rosie kept on stabbing wildly at the button. With a raw growl, he closed his arms round her and the lift doors finally slid shut.

'Let go of me, you caveman!' Rosie splintered breathlessly.

Constantine gazed down at her, blazing golden eyes intent, and splayed hard fingers to the curve of her hip and forced her up against him. That close to that lean, muscular male frame, Rosie froze, bright eyes bewildered as the heat and the scent of him washed over her in a heady, disorientatingly pleasurable tide. A tiny little muscle deep down in her stomach jerked, making her legs feel oddly weak and hollow. Her heart started slamming suffocatingly fast against her ribcage.

'You were trying to flirt with me,' Constantine murmured with a slight frown, his deep, dark drawl sending the most peculiar little shivers travelling down her taut spinal cord. A faint curl of sardonic amusement suddenly quirked his hard mouth.

'Flirt?' Rosie queried in a daze. 'When I threw the wine in your face?'

'You weren't on a winning streak.'

Her bemused gaze connected with molten gold eyes and time seemed to slow down yet move in curious synchronisation with the heavy pounding of the blood in her veins. She struggled to breathe, outrageously conscious of every skin cell in her trembling body, the taut swell of her breasts, the aching sensitivity of her nipples and the straining, melting rush of heat and awareness between her thighs.

No...! she told herself in profound shock. I don't flirt.

As he lowered his arrogant dark head, Constantine smiled lazily, sexily. Rosie was transfixed. His mouth claimed hers with shocking effect. Excitement exploded like a greedy, out-of-control fire inside her, overwhelming her with a voracious passion. She kissed him back in a wild surge of hunger, moaning low in her throat at the stabbing, wickedly erotic intrusion of his tongue. He shifted fluidly against her, making her crave closer contact with a desperation that screamed through every nerve-ending.

He lifted his head to survey her stunned face and drew her out of the lift. Plunged from the breathless heights of unbearable excitement down to the simple business of movement, Rosie met the descent in an agony of disorientation. Inside the suite, he reached for her again with confident hands. The vital energy that flowed from him attracted her like a honey trap. His shimmering golden gaze enveloped her, igniting a floodtide of instinctive heat and response that made her tremble.

'Tell me that you like to make love over and over again,' Constantine invited huskily, his accent roughening the explicit invitation. 'And I will tell you that I will satisfy your every desire.'

Involuntarily, Rosie stiffened and then backed off a shaken step, forcing him to release her again. She felt hideously out of her depth and the shock of that realisation renewed her grasp on reality again. 'I can't sleep with you...' she began shakily.

'Who said anything about sleeping?'

'You said you wouldn't melt,' Rosie reminded him almost accusingly.

'I can melt for one night and repent in the morning...'

'I'm terribly tired... and anyway you have your takeover bid to work at,' Rosie gabbled as it struck her with paralysing force that there was nothing she wanted more, nothing she had *ever* wanted more than she wanted Constantine at that moment, even though every sane sense rebelled and she loathed him with every brain cell she possessed. That was such a devastating truth to face that Rosie was completely floored by it and incapable of retaliating with her usual fire and aggression.

His ebony brows drew together, his soul-destroyingly sensual mouth compressing as a blaze of derision fired his gaze. '*Christos*...I hate women who play sex games! And one night is the only offer I am likely to make,' he delivered with cold clarity. 'I don't pay for sex—'

'And you couldn't *talk* a zombie into it!' Rosie slung at him, feelingly, and stalked into the bedroom, but once she got that door shut her hot face crumpled and her throat convulsed. She leant back weakly while she fought the choking, burning rush of tears dammed up behind her eyelids.

Hours later, Rosie lay awake in the darkness, filled with self-loathing and rampant insecurity. She was still shattered by the sexual response which Constantine had drawn from her. As a teenager she had been subjected to a frightening assault and although she had mercifully emerged from that attack unharmed the encounter had deprived her of any desire to experiment with physical intimacy.

Indeed, growing up, Rosie had developed a deep and abiding distrust of the opposite sex. Furthermore, every time she'd got into a tight corner or felt unhappy she had run away from whatever council home she had been living in. That habit had got her into a lot of trouble until Maurice had convinced her that turning her back on her problems didn't settle them.

All her energies had gone into building up a viable business which would pay the rent. Her need for independence and security had made her drive herself hard. But Anton had cracked her self-sufficiency by persuading her to come down to London. And that was when she had begun to change, opening herself out to emotions and possibilities she had never allowed herself to explore before.

Anton had even dragged her out shopping, making it painfully obvious that he couldn't understand her dislike of feminine clothing, and once again she had given way, helplessly hooked on gaining her father's approval. Tears burned her eyes. Anton had had a struggle to accept her platonic relationship with Maurice. But he had never been able to comprehend the simple fact that most men left her cold. In fact, she would have said that *all* men left her cold... until Constantine Voulos had appeared in that church.

Constantine—the only male she had ever wanted to rip the clothes off and flatten onto the nearest bed. Her cheeks scorched with embarrassment and she scrubbed furiously at her eyes. So that was the power of sexual desire; well, she didn't need him or anyone else to spell out the obvious to her, but nothing could have prepared her for the raw, terrifying strength of that hunger. One kiss and she had gone to pieces like a starstruck groupie.

Thank heaven that after tomorrow she would never, ever see him again. That encounter had meant nothing to Constantine. In the heat of male lust and without even an ounce of liking or respect for her he had offered her a one-night stand. You couldn't get much more sleazy, she thought painfully. He had been tempted but not so tempted that his better judgement hadn't experienced a certain relief when she had turned him down. She had seen that in those surprisingly expressive eyes of his. She grimaced, exhaustion creeping over her like a heavy fog.

Waking with a start, she found Constantine staring down at her. Blinking in the lamplight, Rosie jerked bolt upright, a cold spasm of fear impelling her.

'Do you usually go to bed with all your clothes on?' Constantine enquired, studying the jeans and T-shirt she had put back on.

Taking in the short black robe he was wearing, shaken eyes widening at the slice of bare hair-roughened brown chest that was visible, Rosie leapt out of the other side of the bed.

'*Christos*...what do you think I was about to do? Attack you?' he demanded, openly taken aback by her reaction.

'The sofa is more my size.'

'We can share the bed. It's three in the morning and I have nothing on my mind but an overwhelming desire for sleep,' Constantine asserted with distinct hauteur.

But Rosie closed the bedroom door without answering, traced her way across the dark room beyond and curled up wearily on the sofa. It felt as if she had only just closed her eyes when a loud, persistent knock started hammering on the door. She pushed her tousled head under a cushion and groaned, snuggling into the warmth of a blanket that hadn't been there when she'd gone to sleep. Only when an impatient burst of Greek sounded did she lift her head again.

By then Constantine, clad in close-fitting charcoal-grey trousers and a white silk shirt, was yanking open the door. Dmitri surged in, waving a newspaper and showing every sign of a man throwing a fit. Constantine took the newspaper, exploded briefly back into Greek and then fell silent. Both men turned almost simultaneously to study Rosie...

Caught up in the drama, Rosie stared in wide, innocent enquiry back at them. Constantine opened the door again and the bodyguard departed with unconcealed eagerness. Then Constantine swung back to face Rosie.

'You conniving, cheating little shrew!' he condemned without warning, crossing the room in one long, powerful stride and raising her off the sofa with an even more powerful hand.

'What's the matter with you?' Rosie gasped, shocked by the rage burning in his black, diamond-cutting eyes.

'*Theos*...you will suffer for this!'

'What am I supposed to have done?'

'I was a fool to trust you even this far... My lawyers warned me... why the hell didn't I listen?' Constantine grated, glowering down at her with such loathing and disgust that Rosie turned pale as milk and began to shake, a sick feeling stirring in the pit of her stomach.

He released his hold on her crushed fingers, drew himself up to his full, thoroughly intimidating height and watched her collapse on trembling legs down into the nearest armchair. He lifted a lean brown hand and spread his fingers, the extraordinary force of that single physical gesture capturing her shocked stare.

'You really want to find out what it is like being married to me?' Constantine bit out with a flash of pure fire in his mesmeric, menacing gaze. 'You will wish every minute of every day that you had stayed in your slum dwelling where you belonged and you will be on your knees begging for a divorce before I am finished with you!'

CHAPTER FIVE

WITH extreme difficulty, Rosie snatched in a ragged breath to steady her jumping nerves. 'I still don't know what you're talking about...'

'Don't you *dare* lie to me!' Constantine thundered.

Rosie squinted with fearful curiosity at the newspaper he had flung on the coffee table. Constantine snatched it up again and displayed it like prosecution evidence. TYCOON'S SECRET WEDDING, ran the headline on the front page. Rosie gulped and then gaped at the familiar photograph of herself standing outside the cottage. The last time she had seen that photo, it had been inside a frame on the lounge mantelpiece. It had been taken the day she'd moved in, proud as punch of her first real home since childhood.

'Maurice...' she whispered with pained comprehension, for surely only Maurice could have given that picture to the Press.

'*Maurice,*' Constantine savoured with seething satisfaction. 'I will break him in two!'

'No, it wasn't Maurice!' Rosie gasped in horror, recognising that satisfaction for what it was and even more appalled by the sight of Constantine's clenching fists and rampant aura of physical violence. She coiled her shaking hands together and her tongue stole out to moisten her dry lips. 'It wasn't Maurice... it was *me*.'

'Why try to protect him? He was your accomplice. You must have phoned him to tell him where we were staying because you didn't know our destination until we arrived.'

71

'Yes, I phoned him,' Rosie muttered tightly, and bent her fiery head, the appalling tension in the room tensing her muscles so hard that they ached.

'I presume that you realise what you have done.' His accented drawl fell like a whip, the anger reined back to a chilling coldness which made the tiny hairs at the nape of her neck prickle. 'Thespina will soon know that a wedding has taken place. She has friends in London and she will naturally demand an explanation of my strange failure to inform her of my marriage. Did you think of that...did you even *care*?'

Rosie flinched, tears of strain stinging her eyes.

'No, of course you didn't care. You couldn't see beyond your own greed. Anton left you nothing in his will and you resented that, didn't you?' Constantine condemned with raw-edged distaste. 'No doubt you dreamt of great riches. But two weeks before his death Anton took out a crippling loan to buy a mouldering ruin on the island of Majorca. Sentiment drove him to stake everything he possessed against that single, insane purchase and he was far too proud to approach me for either advice or assistance.'

'Majorca?' Rosie repeated unsteadily, her bright head slowly lifting.

'Son Fontanal, the former Estrada home, complete with contents and a thousand stubbly, infertile acres fit only for a mountain goat,' Constantine recited half under his breath, his lingering incredulity at such a move palpable. 'The ruin even comes complete with an embargo on further development because it stands in an environmentally protected area. It was all but worthless to anyone but Anton. The heirs of the late owner saw him coming...'

'Anton bought back Son Fontanal?' Rosie whispered in breathless shock.

'He was always a deeply sentimental man,' Constantine conceded tautly but with the air of a male striving without success to comprehend such feelings.

But Rosie understood...Rosie understood as if her father had been in the room talking to her. *This* was what Anton had wanted his daughter to have. Son Fontanal, sold out of necessity by his widowed mother when Anton was only fifteen. Her father might have spent the rest of his life in Greece but his deep pain and regret at the loss of his ancestral home had never left him. As a powerless, frustrated teenager, Anton had sworn over his father's grave that if he ever got the chance he would mortgage his soul to bring Son Fontanal back into the family again.

'He loved that house,' Rosie muttered softly. 'No price would have been too high.'

'It was an act of financial suicide. Had he lived...' Constantine's hard mouth clenched, a muscle pulling at the corner of his lips as his deep voice roughened with suppressed emotion. 'Had Anton lived, he would have had a choice between bankruptcy or coming to me. I like to think that he would have overcome his pride and approached me for help—'

'Not his wife?'

Constantine shot her a look of naked disbelief. '*Christos*...what man would want to borrow money from his wife? Why am I discussing these private matters with you?' he grated with sudden ferocity. 'Go and put on that dress you wore last night. We are leaving this hotel.'

'Forget the "we"...I'll call a cab to take me home.'

Constantine loosed a derisive laugh. 'You're coming to Greece with me. That is the only option I have left...and believe me,' he intoned with merciless black eyes, 'if I have to drug you and tie you up to get you there I will do it.'

'G-Greece...?' Rosie stammered incredulously.

'A short meeting with Thespina will be necessary now.'
Constantine dealt her a ferocious look of antipathy.
'That is rather unfortunate when I have already told her
that our fake engagement was broken and that we had
parted.'

'I don't care how you choose to explain yourself but
I am definitely *not* going to Greece,' Rosie assured him
flatly as she got up.

'If necessary I will strip you and dress you myself.'

Rosie collided with black eyes of shamelessly steady
threat. She went into the bedroom. Constantine strode
in after her and detached the phone from its socket.
'From now on you will not be communicating with the
rest of the world. Now get dressed,' he instructed.

Haunted eyes looked back at her from the bathroom
mirror. How could Maurice have done such a dreadful
thing? How could he have contacted the Press? He would
know exactly how she would feel about that betrayal.
He *knew* that she had been determined to protect
Thespina from any further distress. She opened the
bathroom door again and peered out.

Constantine was shrugging his broad shoulders into a
superbly tailored jacket. Her mouth ran dry as she
watched the sleek-toned muscles ripple beneath the fine
silk of his shirt and noted the dark, tantalising shadow
of the hair-roughened chest she had glimpsed during the
night when he'd woken her up.

'Why aren't you changing?' he demanded.

Her cheeks hot as hellfire, Rosie regained her wandering wits and muttered frantically, '*Please* let me phone
Maurice...I have to speak to him.'

Densely lashed dark eyes of outrage landed on her.
'No.'

'Please,' Rosie persisted.

'The first rule of a Greek wife is obedience,' Constantine delivered, moving towards her with the predatory

grace of a prowling leopard. 'And if you don't jump when I say jump, little rag-doll, I will take action to re-educate you and after a very little while in my undiluted company crawling across the floor of my bedroom like a submissive slave will come entirely naturally!'

Rosie slammed the door and locked it for good measure.

'I *can't* go to Greece,' Rosie told him again in the lift.

'I'll content myself with beating Maurice to a pulp and putting him out of business, shall I?' Constantine smiled down at her shaken face. 'And don't you doubt that it can be done. Discreet enquiries have revealed that much as Maurice's old uncle likes his nephew Maurice got his profiteering instincts from the same source, and for the right price Uncle Dennis would regret the necessity but he would shove the pair of you out into the snow!'

Rosie was shattered that Constantine was already aware of the fact that their landlord was related to Maurice. 'You *knew*—?'

'I never make a threat I can't carry through on. You step out of line, I take action in progressive degrees of unpleasantness. I will make Maurice Carter sorry he was ever born and even sorrier that he once shared a bed with you.'

'You're angry...you don't know what you're saying...'

'Anger sharpens my wits but it would appear to scramble yours.'

'Maurice is a completely innocent party in all this.' If Maurice *had* alerted the Press, it could only have been because he genuinely believed that Constantine was trying to cheat her and that publicising their marriage would somehow strengthen her position. In other words, Maurice could only have done it for *her* benefit, so ultimately the responsibility was hers. 'I can't believe that you would want to injure him.'

'Yet you say that Anton told you so much about me.'

Rosie's troubled mind roamed over Anton's frequent descriptive references to Constantine. A ruthless aggressor in business and temperamentally incapable of accepting defeat. A relentless enemy who never forgot a slight, fiercely loyal only to his family, and a male who didn't know what relaxation was...except in the bedroom, women being his one leisure indulgence. Was that how he kept himself so fit?

Colouring, Rosie frowned at her inexcusable loss of concentration and then felt her stomach sinking at the reality of what she had recalled. Her father had loved and admired Constantine for all the qualities that he himself did not possess, she acknowledged wryly. So what did Constantine's enemies have to say about his character?

'This is an evening outfit...I look really stupid in this,' she objected as the cooler temperature of the foyer assailed her bare arms and shoulders.

'You look exactly as I want you to look...like a bimbo who hasn't a clue how to dress in daylight. You don't need to smile for the paparazzi either,' Constantine added as mortified pink erupted over her cheekbones. 'In fact the more miserable and out of place you appear to feel, the less surprised everyone will be when I ditch you again. You see, these rich older guys who bore the pants off their bimbos have a disastrously short attention span for those same bimbos!'

As he led her in the direction of the exit, Rosie was in an agony of teeth-clenching discomfiture. 'Are you saying that there might be reporters outside?'

A split second later, she was confronted with a frightening sea of faces, snapping cameras and shouted questions. As she shivered violently, Constantine doffed his black cashmere overcoat and, draping it round her shoulders with exaggerated gallantry, banded a controlling arm round her spine. He strode silently through the parting crush to the limousine. Nobody got in their way. Rosie was grudgingly impressed by his cool, commanding presence and relieved to see Taki climbing into the front seat beside the chauffeur.

'Are you still planning to sack Taki?' she asked uncomfortably.

'I am still considering the matter.'

'It really wasn't his fault, it was mine.'

Silence rewarded that assurance.

'I can't go to Greece without a passport or clothes,' Rosie pointed out next. 'I'll have to go home first.'

'Dmitri is taking care of that problem. He'll meet us at the airport.'

'I'm hungry.'

'We'll eat on the plane.'

In frustration, Rosie subsided back into the warmth of his overcoat. The rich fabric harboured the faint, elusive male scent of him. Her nostrils flared and she found herself breathing in deeply. Stiffening, she stole a covert glance at him. He was on his mobile phone again but somehow he immediately sensed her surveillance, his long, spiky lashes lifting to reveal compelling dark golden eyes.

Her heart skipped a startled beat but she couldn't break that involuntary connection. Those eyes were extraordinarily arresting in that lean, hard-boned face. His gaze roamed at an outrageously leisurely pace down over the exposed length of her shapely legs. Her skin burned as if he had touched her, her pulses racing wildly. A bitter-sweet ache stirred inside her. It was an effort to breathe as the tension thrummed ever higher between them.

Constantine smiled with sudden raw, earthy amusement, challenging her scrutiny with clear knowledge of the exact effect he was having on her. That awareness shook Rosie inside out. It gave her a shocking foretaste of the very sexual male animal she was dealing with and she was completely unnerved. With a jerk, she turned her head away and flipped his coat hurriedly over her legs.

Constantine threw back his head and laughed.

'Shut up!' Rosie snapped without looking at him.

'You have an astonishing air of innocence,' he murmured silkily. 'I am no longer surprised that Anton fell hook, line and sinker. He was at a dangerous age. It's a shame that he never had the opportunity to see you in your true environment. Only then might he have sensed how false the image was.'

'He had an equally false image of you. He told me that you had great charm, beautiful manners and fascinating conversational skills.' At that point Rosie screened a yawn of boredom with her hand, and was secretly furious and thoroughly disconcerted when Constantine laughed with even greater amusement.

Less than an hour ago, he had been incandescent with rage. But now he *exuded* the indolent cool of a male in supreme control. But he *is* in control, an unwelcome inner voice reminded her. And all, seemingly, because of Maurice. Yet Rosie was still stunned by that apparent betrayal. She had to get her friend on the phone and find out what had really happened. Maybe the photo had been stolen. Maybe the Press had already been on Constantine's trail...

Rosie was deriving precious little pleasure from her first trip abroad. As the car wove through the heavy Athens traffic, she sat rigid-backed and tense at the prospect of having to face Thespina again.

When Dmitri had joined them at the airport with her one suitcase and shabby backpack, she had tried to question him about Maurice but Constantine had prevented her. Since then, her temper had been further exacerbated. On board the private jet she had at least had the opportunity to change into more appropriate clothing but she had then slept through the whole of the flight, waking up only as they landed. By then, having gone without both breakfast and lunch, she had been so hungry that she had been forced to beg Constantine for the appropriate currency with which to buy a bar of chocolate as he'd dragged her through Athens airport, refusing to let her out of his sight for a second.

'If you don't put that blasted phone down, I will scream!' Rosie's hot temper erupted with startling suddenness.

'What is wrong with you now?' Constantine lowered the mobile with the long-suffering aspect of a male dealing with a very tiresome child.

Rosie's teeth gritted. 'I do not want to be involved in telling any more lies to Thespina.'

'Would it give you a bigger kick to walk in and announce yourself as her late husband's mistress?'

Frustration filled her. 'I was *not* Anton's mistress—'

'The mistress who has now become the offensive equivalent of a daughter-in-law? Thespina deserves neither the pain nor the humiliation of that kind of truth,' Constantine countered with fierce emphasis.

The limousine drew up in front of a large, elegant town house. Rosie climbed out into the heat of mid-afternoon, feeling hot, crumpled and sick with nerves. While Constantine spoke to the manservant who had hurried out to greet them, she hung cravenly back behind him.

He swung round and expelled his breath in a stark hiss of pent-up tension.

'Thespina is not here. She flew out to Brazil this morning to stay with friends. Apparently she tried to contact me to let me know her plans but she was unable to reach me.'

A simply huge tide of relief engulfed Rosie. She scooted back into the limousine at speed.

'Now what?' she asked almost brightly.

Constantine frowned. 'It is unlikely that she will hear news of our marriage before her return. Her friends live on a coffee plantation in a remote area.'

'You could phone her.'

'I will wait until I see her. One does not make that sort of announcement on the telephone...' His strong face shuttered.

'So what do we do now?'

Constantine ignored the question. He was in a filthy mood again, Rosie registered. It was not the time to share with him her belief that deception only dug deceivers into a deeper hole. She tried to be fair, tried to ask herself what she would have done in his position. Their secret wedding, designed only to meet the terms of Anton's will, was now a matter of public record. And Constantine's response to that hideous unforeseen development was simply to pretend that he had nothing to hide, indeed that their marriage was a *genuine* marriage...

As that belated acknowledgement finally dawned on Rosie, she turned pale. Earlier in the day, Constantine's fury, her distress over that wretched newspaper article and concern for Maurice and Thespina had blinded her to her own predicament. Now she focused on her companion in open shock. 'You're expecting me to pretend to be your wife?' she whispered in shock.

'You *are* my wife,' Constantine reminded her with driven emphasis.

'Legally speaking, I suppose,' Rosie conceded weakly. 'But— '

'The fiction will have to be maintained for a couple of months at least.'

'I'm a rotten actress. We don't even *like* each other. People aren't so stupid that they're not going to see that!' she protested.

Constantine ignored her again. She hated it when he did that. He closed her out as if she weren't there. It made her feel like an irritating fly he couldn't be bothered to swat.

'I couldn't live with you for one week, never mind a couple of months!'

Constantine shot her a look of naked derision. 'Who do you think you're kidding? You're about to enter bimbo paradise! I have no choice but to keep you in the lap of luxury. But the prospect of rewarding you for your treachery and guile disgusts me!'

Hot-cheeked and seething with resentment, Rosie started practising ignoring *him*. If he fondly imagined she intended to hang around eating humble pie and imitating a wall fixture for the next couple of months, he had another thought coming!

But two hours later, a truly enormous and absolutely delicious meal having brought her back from the edge of starvation, Rosie had a remarkably sunny smile on her formerly disgruntled face. She was lying back in the Jacuzzi in the fabulous bathroom attached to her allotted bedroom. Constantine lived in a breathtakingly beautiful walled estate outside the city. His vast palatial villa swarmed with servants, wondrously keen to ensure that she didn't have to lift a finger to help herself. It was like staying in a five-star luxury hotel.

Admittedly, she had been most uncomfortable when Constantine had introduced her as his blushing bride to the domestic staff. But she had been delirious with delight when she had understood the ramifications of his care in explaining the internal phone system to her. He had informed her that if she *had* to speak to him she was to dial a certain number. He would grow old and

grey waiting for her to call. And in a house this size she
was sure to get hold of a phone with an outside line to
contact Maurice soon. Constantine could not be everywhere simultaneously.

She hated him. And he despised her. So how could
she possibly be attracted to him? Surely that amount of
animosity ought to be a complete turn-off? And why
was that extravagantly gorgeous face of his somehow
etched behind her eyelids like a burr under a saddle?
And why, even though she was frantically glad to finally
be free of his company, could she think of very little
else *but* Constantine? Rosie frowned over that con-
undrum. She felt oddly dislocated... as if she had lost
something, as if she was missing out on something... what, *another* fight?

But, much as it went against the grain, she had to give
him points for some virtues. He clearly adored Thespina.
Seemingly there was nothing that Constantine would not
do to keep her in happy ignorance of her late husband's
last will and testament. And greed had nothing to do
with it. Rosie flushed uncomfortably. Constantine was
every bit as filthy rich as Maurice had said he was. His
private jet, his fantastic home and his lifestyle spoke for
themselves.

He had loved her father too, Rosie conceded reluctantly. Yet they had been such different men with dia-
metrically opposed personalities. Anton had always been
cracking jokes and grinning, looking on the bright side
of every problem and, if possible, cheerfully ignoring
the problem altogether.

Was it easier for Constantine to believe that Anton
had gone off the rails for a young and pretty face? The
truth, she suspected, would be far more damaging.
Anton had kept a big, dark secret from his family for
over twenty years. But then her father had wanted what

he could not have: he had wanted his daughter without hurting his wife.

And although he had often talked about confessing all to Thespina he hadn't been able to grasp that nettle even when he was contemplating his own death. How *could* her father have demanded that Constantine marry her? Rosie shook her head and sighed. Even had Constantine accepted that she was Anton's daughter, her father had had no right to demand such an outrageous sacrifice from his ward.

Wrapped in the towelling robe put there for the purpose, Rosie strolled out of the bathroom, feeling reasonably rested and relaxed. The sensation was short-lived. The bedroom harboured a tall, dark, very masculine intruder.

Rosie tensed, green eyes flying over the Italian-styled double-breasted beige suit Constantine was wearing. It gave him the look of a stunningly sexy and dangerous gangster. For a split second, he quite took her breath away and she was transfixed. That sensation didn't last either.

Constantine frowned at her. 'Did I not make it clear that for the duration of your stay here you were to behave as if this was a normal marriage?'

Uncertainly, Rosie nodded.

'Then why did you insist on dining from a tray instead of joining me downstairs for dinner? And why did you refuse my housekeeper's offer to give you a guided tour of the villa?'

Rosie heaved a stoical sigh. 'Anything else I've done wrong?'

'You're not a guest here. This is supposed to be your home. Act like a newly married woman.'

'I haven't a clue how a newly married woman acts.'

'But you have an incredible imagination. *Use it*,' Constantine suggested with sardonic bite.

It was already being used. In her mind's eye, Constantine had mysteriously become a brooding gangster from a shadowy old black and white movie. And mysteriously sharing that same scene *was* ... Rosie, garbed in a fabulous fringed twenties dress, the sole focus of her gangster's seething passions. Emerging in shock from her first experience of erotic fantasy, Rosie drew in a tumultuous, steadying breath and wondered frantically what was going on inside her head.

'What's the matter with you? You're unusually quiet.' Constantine ran suspicious black eyes over her.

'Jet lag,' Rosie said shrilly, embarrassed to death by that sexual daydream.

'I'll see if I can arrange a flight for you *every* day,' Constantine drawled without a flicker of a smile on his way out of the door.

While she had been in the Jacuzzi her luggage had been unpacked but Rosie was surprised to see her little brocade jewel case sitting on the dressing-table. In fact, having already had an unhappy preview of the collection of motley garments Maurice had tumbled willy-nilly into the case, she was astonished that he had been thoughtful enough to pack her jewellery into the backpack.

Opening it, she frowned and then poked through several sets of tangled costume beads in an increasingly desperate search for what she had expected to find. Her heart stopped dead and her stomach literally heaved. *The Estrada ring was no longer there* ... and Rosie lost no time in jumping to the most obvious conclusion. Constantine had been determined to take that ring from her. And, lo and behold, it was now gone! Obviously Constantine had stolen her father's gift from her!

Rosie raced down the long, sweeping staircase barefoot. The light of battle in her furious gaze, she saw Constantine emerging from a room off the huge hall. 'I want my ring back!' she slung at him full volume.

Startled, Constantine wheeled round to face her. 'What the hell—?'

'The Estrada ring. It was in my jewel case. Now it's gone.'

'Gone?' Constantine stressed as he curved a hand round one slight shoulder and pressed her into an elegant reception room. 'Gone where?'

Rosie grimaced. 'I was hoping you wouldn't do this.'

'If you've lost that ring,' Constantine spelt out rawly, 'I'll strangle you!'

'The best line of defence being attack, right?' Rosie looked deeply cynical and her lip curled. 'Look, I know you have the ring and that you are responsible for its disappearance—'

'Christos . . . do you dare to accuse *me* of stealing?' Constantine flared in outrage.

Rosie winced and backtracked a diplomatic inch or two. 'I wouldn't use that term. Let's just say that you have retrieved something which you believe I have no right to retain. But I have every right. Anton *gave* me that ring.'

'I am not a thief. If the emerald is missing we will call the police, but not until I am fully convinced that this is not another ploy.'

'Ploy . . . what's that supposed to mean?' Rosie splintered.

'It means,' Constantine stated with hauteur, 'that I would not at all be surprised to learn that your boyfriend has the ring. I'm already well aware that you're a liar and a cheat—'

'You swine!' Rosie gasped with a shudder of disbelief.

'And I imagine the ring is heavily insured—'

At that instant, a servant came to the door and spoke to Constantine while Rosie stood with balled fists of fury.

His arrogant dark head turned. 'You'll have to excuse me. I have a visitor.'

For the space of three minutes, Rosie was frozen to the carpet by that careless dismissal. Either Constantine didn't believe that the ring was genuinely missing or he was being very clever in his pretence of distrust and ignorance. He had to be lying—he *had* to be! Her restive gaze fell on the telephone and stilled. Only then did it occur to her that she didn't know the international code for the UK. A minute search of the room revealed no directory. She didn't even know how to dial the operator in Greece, so how could she contact Maurice?

Frustration currenting through her in a wild surge, she marched out into the hall again and then hesitated, frowning as she heard voices. Constantine and his visitor. His late caller was female and, surprisingly, English. Curiosity took her to the ajar door. She glanced in.

'Louise...' Constantine was saying very, very drily.

A gorgeous brunette with legs as long as rail tracks and even better exposed was reclining on a chaise longue, making very unconvincing play with a frilly handkerchief.

'But to read something like *that* in a newspaper... I was devastated, Constantine! How could you get married without telling me? You said you wouldn't be marrying for years and years and I'm really not at all sure that I can find it within myself to continue as your mistress now that you have a wife,' Louise moaned in a petulant lament, flicking back her glamorous dark mane of hair while her steel-blue gaze carefully judged her effect on the target of her complaints.

Unfortunately that target was out of Rosie's view but that did not inhibit her. Eyes sparkling like emerald gemstones, Rosie pressed the door back and planted herself on the threshold. 'I think I can help you to make up your mind,' she murmured sweetly. 'Come within one hundred yards of Constantine again and I will scratch your eyes out!'

The brunette reared up in comical shock. Constantine spun round, black eyes aflame with sheer incredulity.

'As for *you*,' Rosie breathed, folding her arms with undeniable enjoyment in her role and fixing her full attention on her fake husband, who curiously felt rather more like a husband than he had yet, 'I suggest you remove your ladyfriend from *my* home immediately... because I never make a threat I can't carry through on.'

At the repetition of his own words of earlier in the day, Constantine turned pale beneath his bronzed skin. An incandescent blaze of gold shimmered in his eyes before he veiled them, his sensual mouth compressing into a bloodless line of self-restraint. Constantine silenced. Well, well, well, how the mighty have fallen, Rosie savoured without pity.

The brunette strolled out provocatively slowly past Rosie. She was about a foot taller. Then she paused and glanced back with a curious malicious smile in Constantine's direction. 'It may seem a strange thing to say in the circumstances but your little jailbait bride has just made my day. Why do I get this feeling that life as you know it is over? She'll give you hell and you *deserve* it!'

Rosie watched Louise depart, secretly impressed to death by her cool, dignified exit. As a door slammed in the distance, she sighed, 'I'm so glad you didn't break her heart. Well, how did I do?'

The silence pulsed as if it were about to explode.

'*How... did... you... do?*' Constantine framed between audibly grinding teeth.

'In the newly married woman stakes... was I convincing? I mean, there is just no way a wife would walk past a scene like that in her own home. As you reminded me, I am *not* just a guest here.'

Constantine swung away from her and spread lean brown hands in an unsteady arc of scantily leashed rage. She had the feeling that he couldn't quite believe what had just happened to him. He swore raggedly half under his breath in his own language. Then he murmured, not quite levelly. 'Do you have a single sensitive bone in your body?'

Rosie shook her fiery head. 'Not where you're concerned. I was a bit worried that I might be reading the signals wrong and that your ladyfriend might be sincerely attached to you. But she wasn't, was she? So no harm done.'

'You did it quite deliberately. I am preventing you from contacting that prehistoric ape Maurice and in return you decided to start screwing up *my* private life.'

'Newly married men don't have private lives.'

'You think not?' Constantine purred like a big jungle cat as he prowled round her in an ever-shrinking circle of intimidation. 'Are *you* not a part of my private life? Have you not forced me to acknowledge you as my wife?'

Rosie suffered a sudden alarming loss of confidence, for the first time wishing she hadn't been quite so eager to confess to sins she hadn't committed earlier in the day. 'Constantine—'

'What?'

Rosie took a tiny backward step, her heart thumping somewhere in the region of her throat. 'I think it's time I went to bed.'

'So do I.' Constantine closed his arms deftly around her slim frame and swept her off her feet.

'What do you think you're doing?' Rosie shrieked.

'What I should have done last night!' Constantine started up the stairs with determination.

'Put me down! Have you gone crazy?'

'It's your own bloody fault! *Christos* . . . you keep on pushing and pushing!' Constantine roared down at her

accusingly. 'I put you in a room as far away from me
as I could get you and still keep you under the same
roof! I was determined not to be tempted by you again.
I have tried to keep my distance—'

'Well, you're not trying very hard now, are you?' Rosie
snapped back tempestuously. 'And if you don't let go
of me right this minute I'm going to hit you so hard
you'll be knocked into the middle of next week!'

'Your mouth is bigger than you are,' Constantine
growled, his deep voice thickening in a manner that sent
Rosie's self-preserving instincts shooting to full power.
'Why not kiss me instead?'

'Because I don't want to kiss you!'

'No?'

'Do I look that dumb?' Rosie spat.

But then Constantine blocked out the light with the
hot, hungry heat of his mouth, and the world spun so
violently, she gasped and clutched at him. Electrifying
heat engulfed her... or maybe it was him. He seemed to
be burning up too. Her fingers framed his hard cheekbones and her head went back as he knotted one hand
tightly into her hair and kissed her with bruising, demanding thoroughness until she thought she would pass
out from lack of oxygen but didn't care because nothing
had ever felt so good.

In darkness he brought her down on a bed, and as he
released her mouth with a stifled groan of frustration
she lay there winded and gasping in air like a drowning
swimmer. A light went on and she blinked dazedly.
Constantine came down on the bed beside her, wrenching
at his silk tie, shrugging out of his jacket. *Run,* a little
voice urged her. But she clashed with eyes of searing
gold and her whole body turned liquid and unfamiliar,
her mind blanking out as an uncontrollable surge of
hunger overwhelmed her.

'Don't lie there like a sacrifice, you little witch,' he breathed unevenly. 'Don't let me think...I only want to *feel*—'

His hand wasn't quite steady as he tugged her up to him again. Intense satisfaction filled her, along with a heady sense of power. She snatched in the husky male scent of him so close and every sense thrilled, a desperate wanting that overpowered inhibition driving her hand up to sink wonderingly into the silky black depths of his hair. A tenderness that was new to her made her heart twist and her fingers tremble and his ebony brows drew together in a frown that might have been surprise.

He leant forward and let the tip of his tongue dip between her lips in a heart-stoppingly erotic foray. She shivered violently and then reached for him because she couldn't help herself, finding his carnal mouth again, and instantly he took charge with a husky growl of dominance, kissing her until she was a quivering mass of aching nerve-endings.

A lean hand jerked at the tie on the towelling robe and then closed over one small, pouting breast. The sensation of pleasure was so intense, Rosie almost had a cardiac arrest.

Lifting his dark, tousled head, Constantine smiled sexily down into her shaken face. 'You like that?'

Rosie didn't have words to tell him how much. She was lost in another world, a wholly physical place where only sensation ruled. He sent his tongue skimming over a swollen pink nipple and her back arched, her teeth clenching, her nails clawing into the bedspread beneath her. All she knew was that she wanted more, more of that stunning, heart-racing pleasure, and only he could give it. He lowered his head and tasted her supersensitive flesh and she jerked and whimpered, experiencing a pleasure that blew her mind and reduced her to trembling, gasping submission.

'*Christos* . . . you're hot,' Constantine groaned, lowering his big, powerful body and shuddering as his hands sank to the swell of her hips, forcing her into contact with the hard, swollen evidence of his arousal and then rolling back from her with a curse of frustration, an impatient hand flying to the belt-buckle of his trousers.

Hot . . . *hot*? Rosie tensed, her brain flying back into gear. She squinted down at the shameless thrust of her bare breasts, still glistening damply from his lovemaking. For an instant she was frozen there, at a peak of appalled horror that almost equalled her former pitch of excitement, and then she was off that bed so fast, she could have challenged and outrun an Olympic sprinter.

'*Theos* . . . *!*' Incredulity exploded from Constantine and took his fluent English with it as he vented a flood of guttural Greek.

Rosie fled into the dark corridor like a lemming charging suicidally at a cliff. *Hot* . . . cheap, easy, sordid. Dear heaven, how had she let him get that far? One minute she had been shouting at him and the next . . . Typical Constantine manoeuvre: hit on her one vulnerability and try to use her to level the score. Turn a pitched battle into a sexual orgy and then smirk with macho male superiority. She shuddered in disgust and then registered in horror that the corridor had come to a dismaying dead end.

Constantine stopped ten feet away in a patch of moonlight. Rosie whipped back against the wall, arms spread in sudden instinctive fear, her slender length braced for attack.

'What the hell *is* this?'

'Don't you dare t-touch me . . .' Her voice was a sick thread of sound.

Constantine stared, incisive black eyes pinned to her frightened face. 'I'm not a rapist,' he said grimly. 'I can take a refusal without becoming violent.'

Trembling, still not quite trusting him, Rosie let her arms slide heavily down the wall and curved them protectively round herself instead, agonisingly aware that she had exposed more than her body to him now in betraying that fear. And a part of her was already acknowledging that she had behaved badly. Lying all but naked on a bed with him and responding with such wild abandon had given him every reason to react incredulously to her sudden change of heart.

'Watching a woman cringe from me as if I am about to attack her has to be the equivalent of ten cold showers at once,' Constantine completed flatly, his nostrils flaring.

'I didn't think you were about to—' she began shakily.

'You *did* think that.'

But only at the height of her appalled turmoil about what had so nearly happened between them. When she had seen him poised there against the darkness, that old subconscious fear had rushed to the surface in response to the sheer physical threat of his masculine power and size.

'I have never had to use force to bed a woman. Nor would I,' Constantine asserted with raw-edged hauteur.

'I led you on...I'm sorry,' Rosie mumbled, frantically wishing he would just go away and leave her to recover in privacy.

'Why?'

That one bald question made Rosie squirm. There was only one answer but it was not an answer she wished to give. Swallowing hard on her reluctance, she muttered, 'I wanted you...' And admitting that to *him* was like drinking a cup of poison.

'Then...?' Constantine prompted without pity.

Her face was now burning so hot, she was convinced she was glowing in the dark like a neon light.

'When you're trying to shrink into a wall, it is a challenge to see you as a natural-born tease, and you *did* almost hit the ceiling in your haste to vacate that hotel bed last night. For a woman with a chequered past, you're strangely nervous when it comes to sex.'

Rosie imagined telling him that she was a virgin and as quickly discarded the mortifying notion with an inner shudder. He wouldn't believe her. He couldn't know how utterly terrifying it was to find herself at the mercy not only of feelings and sexual responses that were new to her, but also at the mercy of a sophisticate like him and realise that she had completely lost control. Constantine made a sensual, seductive feast of lovemaking. Never mind those startlingly eye-catching dark good looks, what about the incredible technique?

Blushing all over again, Rosie forced her dry lips apart and said, 'We don't even like each other.'

'That has a strange, perverse appeal all of its own.'

Rosie swallowed with difficulty at that disturbing assertion.

Constantine watched her with eyes that glittered like diamonds in the moonlight. 'You're running scared, aren't you?' he murmured with sudden amusement.

'I don't understand.'

'You're a control freak and I have found your self-destruct button. I have no doubt that you kept Anton and the throwback spinning in separate orbits with the greatest of ease—'

'The throwback?'

'Maurice...the label fits him like a glove. A great hulking thicko, whose only talent is inbred cunning for enriching himself,' Constantine extended smoothly.

'Maurice is not thick!' Rosie hissed furiously.

'Of course he is. He's pushed you into my arms. Does he really believe that you'll go back to him after being with me and living in my world?'

'I'm not going to *be* with you in any sense!'

'But the throwback is history. Anton is dead. And you are Mrs Constantine Voulos...for the moment.' Constantine swung on his heel and glanced back at her. 'I won't have to wait long for you to fall into my bed. I would say you are physically incapable of staying out of it!'

He had almost disappeared into the darkness when Rosie raked in an infuriated tone, 'How do I get back to my room?'

Constantine spun round, flung his darkly handsome head back and laughed with raw and unconcealed appreciation of her plight. Rosie thrust shaking hands into her pockets and boiled with loathing. In silence because she didn't trust herself to speak, they reached the relevant corridor.

'I know where I am now.'

'Do you?' His intonation suggested a deeper meaning.

Rosie stiffened, her breath catching in her throat as he curved a staying arm round the base of her slender spine. Raising his hand, he caught a single corkscrew curl and watched with gleaming satisfaction as it coiled obediently round one lean brown forefinger.

Black eyes skimmed direct to hers. 'You're not as tough as you like to make out, are you? In fact, you're on the brink of panic...but think of the potential rewards. Please me and you won't ever have to sell yourself to an older man again!'

Rosie stumbled into her bedroom like a drunk. She was shaking all over. It had been many years since anyone had made her feel weak and powerless. But Constantine had achieved that feat within thirty-six hours. And she wasn't just on the brink, she *was* panicking, with her life suddenly resembling an accident black spot and Constantine continuing to come at her like a particularly deadly juggernaut moving in for the kill.

He had found her Achilles heel and he was already starting to work out what made her tick. She had been a complete fool to keep on challenging a male as sexually experienced as Constantine. And if she ended up in bed with a man who despised her how would she feel about herself then? Wouldn't it be nice to think that she could resist her own most basic urges?

But then it was *him* she couldn't seem to resist. Ignorant, arrogant, macho, *clever* swine that he was. Little rag-doll—oh, yes, she had been behaving just like a little rag-doll. A toy he could push around and play with. And maybe once or twice she had succeeded in outfacing Constantine, but ultimately she had ended up paying very dearly for the privilege.

Why had Anton never warned her that Constantine could be so terrifyingly unpredictable? Or that beneath those smooth, expensive clothes beat the heart and soul of a very primal and passionate male whose every instinct was ruthlessly grounded on a need not only to win but to dominate?

And what about the *other* women in his life? Louise, the mistress, emotionally detached but vindictive enough to delight in the belief that another woman might be giving Constantine his comeuppance at last…and exactly where did the beautiful Italian actress, Cinzia Borzone, who was supposedly his only true love, fit in? Rosie was suddenly even more appalled by her own shameless, reckless behaviour. Evidently Constantine had few morals. And she herself had very nearly fallen victim to his magnetic sexuality as well.

It was time she used the brain she had been born with. Why *should* she have to stay in Greece? It would be madness to risk another uneasy meeting with Thespina. Constantine would simply have to tell her that his bride had already left him. He could even truthfully add that his wife had had a surprise meeting with his mis-

tress...exit wife. Exit where? It didn't take Rosie two
minutes to work out the most desirable destination. She
would go to Majorca to see Son Fontanal before Constantine sold it again.

An hour later, weighed down only by her backpack,
Rosie was lowering herself off the balcony outside her
room. She made a slight detour onto a drainpipe to reach
the sturdy climber covering the wall and then descended
as sure-footed as a cat down onto the paved terrace
below. Somewhere too close for comfort, a dog barked.
Rosie took off at speed across the landscaped gardens,
dodging and weaving like a professional. There was more
than one dog barking now and her adrenalin hit an all-
time high. As she got near the perimeter wall, some sort
of siren screamed and suddenly a man appeared out of
the darkness.

Rosie made a rush at the wall. The man got in the
way. On the brink of her kicking him, he coughed and
she recognised him. 'Taki...?'

He froze in astonishment.

'Taki, *please*,' she pleaded as the dogs got closer.

He gave her a leg-up over the ten-foot wall. By then
another alarm was screeching in tune with the siren. Rosie
dropped down onto the road and then scudded across
it into the cover of some bushes. A police car with a
flashing light wheeled to a screeching halt as the elec-
tronic gates sprang open. Rosie set off up the road. Eat
your heart out, Rambo, she thought smugly. But
Constantine really ought to employ Taki elsewhere. Taki
was too impressionable for Constantine's safety.

Why the heck should she care? Well, she might be
putting as much distance as she possibly could between
herself and Constantine but she didn't want anything
really bad to happen to him. Her father had been very

fond of him. As for her, well, Constantine had taken the ring and severed their agreement. He was on his own now, and so was she, and that was just the way Rosie liked it.

CHAPTER SIX

'WHERE the blazes are you?' Maurice bawled at deafening volume down the line.

Rosie held the telephone at a distance from her ear. 'Majorca—'

'*Majorca?* What the blinkin' heck are you doing there? Constantine's been here...he was frantic! Hell, Rosie, you might have at least left the poor bloke a note! He—'

'Since when did you start feeling sorry for Constantine?' Rosie interrupted in an incredulous hiss.

'Since I saw him demonstrating serious concern for your whereabouts and welfare,' Maurice informed her with nauseating piety. 'You're abroad for the first time in your life, you don't speak the lingo, you don't have any money *and* you disappeared from his home in the middle of the night. I thought you'd grown out of doing moonlit flits.'

'It wasn't like that.' But Rosie flushed furiously.

'Constantine was hopping mad when he arrived because he was so certain you would be here with me. But when he found out that you weren't he started panicking.'

'Constantine is not the panicking type—'

'Where did you get the money to take yourself to Majorca?'

'Never mind that, I want to know *how*—'

'Where are you staying? I'm coming over.'

'Don't be ridiculous—'

'I'm fed up with you and Constantine raving about the globe like a couple of hot-tempered, irrational lunatics. Last time I saw him he was mobilising the Greek police to look for you! If you don't tell me where you're staying, I'll tell *him* you're in Majorca—'

Five seconds later, Rosie slammed out of the phone box without even having found out how the news of the wedding had got into the hands of the Press. It upset her to be at loggerheads with Maurice but it was time that he appreciated that she was no longer the terrified thirteen-year-old he had once saved from sexual assault. She clambered back onto the motorbike she had hired, trying not to think with miserly regret about the secret rainy-day account she had more than half-emptied in the space of three days.

Her sparkling eyes hardened as she rode out of the sleepy little village and back onto the endless mountain road with its perilous bends and truly terrifying drops. Knowing that Constantine had flown over to England in pursuit of her made her feel hunted. It infuriated her too. Little more than a month ago she had not even met the swine and now he was acting as if he owned her! So what if she had fled imprisonment in the middle of the night? She had done what she had agreed to do in marrying him and he had no right, no right whatsoever, to try and demand any further sacrifices from her!

By mid-morning, Rosie was studying a battered iron name-plate hanging by a piece of barbed wire from a set of seriously rusty gates. Son Fontanal appeared to lie up a rutted cart track that climbed a steep hill thickly wooded with pines. Half an hour later, having abandoned the motorbike under the trees, Rosie gazed down at her father's birthplace in the fertile valley below and caught her breath in enchantment.

The villa had a faded red roof and ageless peach-coloured stone walls, the twin wings of the two-storey building joined by a graceful loggia supported on pillars lushly entwined by a giant jacaranda. Furthermore there appeared to be a more passable paved laneway running to the rear of the building. On the south side, a series of crumbling arches ran round the perimeter of an overgrown garden studded with palm trees. Not crumbling, just *old*, Rosie adjusted hurriedly, and maybe there were a few roof tiles missing here and there and a few cracks on the walls...but no way was Son Fontanal the ruin which Constantine had called it!

She hurried down the sloping track, her steps only slowing as she approached the courtyard entrance. A plump elderly lady was dozing on a chair in the shade cast by the loggia. As Rosie drew closer, wondering how on earth she was to introduce herself, the old woman woke up and fixed startled eyes on her. Then her creased face slowly blossomed into a beam of positive pleasure.

Rising with surprising vigour, she opened her arms almost as if she was expecting Rosie to rush into them. 'Señorita Estrada?' she exclaimed.

Being addressed by her father's name made Rosie still in astonishment. A torrent of Spanish broke over her as the old lady surged forward to clasp her hands and kiss her warmly on both cheeks. Tears shone in her dark eyes. From the pocket of her pristine white apron, she withdrew a rather crumpled photograph. *'La hija de Don Antonio*...the daughter of Don Antonio,' she sighed, proudly displaying a snapshot of Anton and Rosie together. 'I am Carmina...'

Carmina, once her father's nursemaid. Rosie realised that she needed no further introduction. This old lady actually *knew* who she was. When Anton had flown in to buy Son Fontanal, he had found Carmina still in residence, and in the emotional grip of that reunion and homecoming he had clearly confessed that he had a daughter. Rosie's own eyes stung and a tremulous smile of happiness curved her lips. It meant so much to her that her father had confided in someone about her existence.

The old woman went back into her pocket and produced a carefully folded piece of newspaper and slowly shook her grey head. 'No señorita...señora,' Carmina stressed with a cheerful smile of self-reproof. 'Señora Voulos...yes?'

Bloody hell, Rosie thought, limp with incredulity and resentment. Halfway up a mountain in a foreign country, she *still* couldn't shake off Constantine and the consequences of that stupid wedding ceremony! Speaking in an excitable mix of Spanish and increasingly confident English now, Carmina went on to enquire anxiously as to the whereabouts of her *esposo*...Spanish for husband, Rosie gathered, her teeth gritting. And almost simultaneously a distant humming noise in the background broke like a thunderclap over the brow of the steep hill she had climbed. Frowning, she looked heavenward.

A scarlet helicopter hung like a giant brash bird against the cloudless blue sky. Rosie left the courtyard to watch the craft circling in search of a landing place. It came down about fifty yards away on the flat ground to the front of the villa. Even before the rotor blades had stopped twirling, a large male figure sprang out. Rosie's heart sank and then gave a paradoxically violent lurch of excitement that interfered with her ability to breathe and filled her with appalled and ashamed discomfiture.

Constantine powered towards her on long, lean, muscular legs. Rosie skidded off one foot onto the other, accidentally clashed with blazing, implacable black eyes and froze, caught like a butterfly pinned live to a specimen board. 'I—' she began in an odd, squeaky, breathless voice she didn't recognise as her own.

As Constantine drew level with her, he stopped dead. Without the smallest warning, he bent and swept her off her feet into his arms. Rosie was silenced by complete shock.

'What I have to say to you does not require an audience,' Constantine splintered in a menacing undertone. 'And isn't it traditional to carry the bride over the threshold?'

Rosie's last view of the helicopter took in Dmitri, whose rock-like visage usually defied interpretation. Not on this occasion, however. Constantine's bodyguard wore a huge appreciative grin.

Scarlet-cheeked, Rosie spat, 'Put me down!'

'*Make me,*' Constantine challenged, stalking through the open doors of Son Fontanal.

Rosie struck his back with two outraged fists.

'You'll have to do better than that, little rag-doll—'

'Don't call me that...I *hate* it!' she launched at him as he started up a wide stone staircase.

'But it is *so* appropriate. If I was the kind of husband you deserve, I would be on the happy brink of beating the stuffing out of you!'

'What's that supposed to mean?' Rosie gasped.

'That I have to come up with another method of punishment—and I have had plenty of time to toy with several interesting possibilities, haven't I?' Constantine murmured in a sizzling purr of threat as he thrust open a carved door. 'In three nightmare days, I have flown from Athens to Manchester, from Manchester to London and from London back to Athens...and then from Athens to Palma. I want someone to pay in spades for that travel itinerary.'

'I don't know why you bothered—'

'Do you want to know what kept me going?' Constantine yanked her off his shoulder, tossed her in the air to clamp two incredibly strong hands beneath her arms and then held her in suspension, face to menacing face. Rosie's immediate surroundings shrank to her own shocked and tiny mirror image in a pair of implacable, glittering black eyes.

'No...' she whispered, dry-mouthed and hypnotised.

'The thought of this moment,' Constantine spelt out not quite evenly as she gazed back at him like a mesmerised rabbit. 'When I show you how a Greek husband treats a runaway wife—'

'Not your wife...' Rosie fumbled with great difficulty to find that disjointed denial. Her brain felt for all the world as though it was set in cement. Not a single rational thought clouded her head. The warm, musky scent of him overlaid with a faint hint of some citrusy aftershave floated into her flaring nostrils, and the more she breathed, the more dizzy and peculiar she felt.

Constantine's intent gaze flashed pure scorching gold. He murmured something rough in Greek and settled her down on the big carved bed that she hadn't even noticed. She sat up again very slowly, her legs and arms oddly unresponsive to her bidding.

Constantine reached down a hand, flipped her gently back against the heaped-up white linen pillows and grated, 'Stay there!'

Rosie stayed put. Wide-eyed, she watched him discard his tie, his jacket and rip at his silk shirt with scant concern for the buttons. Her tongue was welded to the roof of her mouth. A disturbing tremor ran through her tautening length. Her entire attention was nailed to Constantine's bare chest, her spellbound gaze wandering from the gleaming brown skin of his shoulders to the black triangle of curling hair hazing his powerful pectoral muscles.

It was so hard to breathe, even harder to keep her fingers curling into her palms when this insane part of her craved the freedom to shift forward a mere foot to the edge of the bed and *touch*...run exploring fingertips over that smooth golden skin, investigate the un-

deniable allure of that hard, flat stomach and that truly
fascinating little silky furrow of dark hair which started
just below his navel and travelled all the way down until
it disappeared under the low-slung edge of a pair of black
briefs. He was just in the act of hooking a finger into
those briefs when Rosie realised in horror that she was
gawping at him like a woman at a male strip show.

'Take your clothes off,' Constantine said.

Rosie had twisted her head away so fast, she was all
but suffering from whiplash, face as hot as a furnace,
gut feelings of shame and shock reverberating through
her blitzed brain. So he had a really beautiful body. Was
that any excuse to behave like a peeping Tom? But it
was even worse to recognise the swollen heaviness of her
breasts and the hot liquid sensation of unforgivable excitement burning somewhere she didn't even want to
think about. *What* had he said?

Constantine saved her the trouble of plundering her
dazed mind for recollection. He said it again. Her bright
head whipped back as fast as the head of a swivelling
doll, huge green eyes agog at the command.

'OK,' Constantine gritted with savage impatience, and
reached for her in one alarmingly fast motion.

'What are you doing?' Rosie screeched as her over-
sized T-shirt went flying over her startled head and he
anchored a businesslike hand into the elasticised
waistband of her leggings. Preoccupied by an instinctive
need to cover her braless breasts with spread fingers, she
was decidedly hampered in the undignified tussle which
followed. Her leggings and her briefs were wrenched off
together to the accompaniment of her aghast shrieks and
breathless and impotent efforts to fight him off.

Clamping a hand like an iron vice to her forearm,
Constantine held her fast and flipped the sheet over her
frantically struggling body. Sliding into the bed with her,
he rolled over and anchored an arm round her waist and

yanked her back into electrifying contact with his hot, muscular masculinity. Rosie went rigid. He wasn't wearing a stitch and neither was she and she just could not *believe* that he had forcibly stripped her naked!

'I'll go to the police and report you for this the minute I get out of this room!' Rosie gasped the instant she got oxygen back into her straining lungs.

'Be sure to tell them that I am your husband. I should think they'll laugh themselves sick—'

'You are *not* my husband!' Rosie spat with renewed vigour. 'And if you dare to lay a finger on me—'

'Shut up and go to sleep,' Constantine growled, spreading his big, powerful body across the bed with a deep, luxuriating groan of contentment and forcing her to move with him.

'G-go to sleep?' Rosie queried shakily, every fibre of her trembling body centred in awareness on the bold thrust of his erection against her slender hip.

'I have not slept more than a handful of hours in the past three days. So when I sleep *you* sleep too,' Constantine told her, his deep, dark drawl winding audibly down in speed and volume.

Rosie twisted round in the manacle-like imprisonment of his arm. In a bewildered daze, she surveyed him. His drowsy eyes were darkly shadowed, the crescent lashes as long and luxuriant as a child's already in the act of drifting down towards his cheekbones. Close up, she noticed how pale he was. As she recalled the travel schedule he had outlined, the strangest little pang of guilt nudged at her conscience and provoked a deep flush on her troubled face.

'You don't trust me not to disappear again,' she gathered tautly. 'But I'm prepared to promise that I'll still be in this house when you wake up.'

In unconvinced response, Constantine shifted and snaked his other arm beneath her, forcing her even closer and into, if possible, an even more disturbing intimacy because this time she was facing him and lying half over the outrageously relaxed sprawl of his abrasively masculine frame.

'*Constantine...!*' Rosie shrieked in anguish as he crushed her breasts into the solid wall of his hair-roughened chest and pushed her head down under his chin.

'If you keep me awake I'll get amorous,' he warned her thickly. 'I like to make love before I sleep. Sex is a wonderful antidote to stress and tension, *pethi mou*.'

There was only one tense person in the bed after that assertion and it wasn't Constantine.

Rosie lay as still as a statue with the slow, steady beat of his heart thudding against her breast and the deep rise and fall of his breathing stirring her hair. He had both arms wrapped round her in an entirely asexual embrace. Indeed she might as well have been an inanimate toy. He had dragged her into bed with him only to ensure that she did not get the chance to make a break for freedom again. Now he was sleeping like a big, happy, contented log!

In dismaying contrast, Rosie was in a state of turmoil which was becoming horribly familiar to her in Constantine's radius. Pure panic had provoked her flight from Greece. She winced at the awareness. Even asleep, Constantine reacted to that slight movement of hers, his arms tightening round her as he rolled over, pinning one long, powerful thigh between hers. Her taut nipples throbbed and her stomach clenched with horrendous excitement, her treacherous body responding with a brazen life and hunger all of its own. Rosie simply wanted to *die* of mortification.

He had ripped off her clothes and she had experienced not one decent pang of fear. She had been outraged but not scared and, worst of all, when he had told her to go to sleep she had been shattered and then…and then…*disappointed*? A sexual craving that horrified her still hungered like a wicked beast inside her. And she felt even more threatened by the discovery that one glimpse of Constantine looking exhausted could make her feel guilty and strangely sympathetic. How could she feel guilty about a male she loathed? Where had all her anger gone?

Shaken awake in an only vaguely familiar bedroom, Rosie slowly lifted her head off the pillow she was hugging, bemused eyes landing on Constantine. Fully dressed, he was standing by the bed, every vibrant battery blatantly recharged, energy sizzling from him in intimidating waves. He looked incredibly gorgeous.

'What time is it?' she mumbled, disorientated by the daylight still flooding through the windows and then deeply disturbed by the realisation that she had actually managed to fall asleep in his arms. True, she had not slept a great deal herself in recent days, but that was no excuse for relaxing to *that* extent.

'Three in the afternoon. It's time for you to get up. Lunch is being prepared.'

'By whom…Carmina?' she muttered round a still sleepy yawn as she stretched.

'Since I was aware that the house had only an elderly caretaker in residence, I arranged for a number of my staff to follow me here,' Constantine supplied drily. 'But since habitable rooms are at a premium they'll be using the holiday cottages on the edge of the estate.'

Sitting up, Rosie carefully hugged the sheet to her collarbone. Without shame, Constantine stared. A rosy red blush started at her breasts and crawled up her throat before she hurriedly broke back into speech. 'How the heck did you find out where I was?'

'The passenger manifest of your flight. Is this trip meant to be some sort of sentimental journey?' Constantine dealt her a stonily unimpressed appraisal, openly suspicious as to why she should have chosen to take refuge in Anton's family home.

'I thought it would be the last place you would look for me.' Rosie ducked her head, her eyes clouding. A sentimental journey...if only he knew. But then he didn't know and he had shot her down in flames when she had tried to tell him who she was. His contemptuous dismissal of her claim had bitten deep.

'Where is your wedding ring?' Constantine demanded so abruptly that she jumped.

'I took it off.'

'Then put it back on again,' Constantine told her grimly.

'I can't...' Rosie shrugged. 'I dropped it in a bin when I got off the plane at Palma.'

Constantine slowly breathed in and slowly breathed out again. Rosie recognised the exercise for what it was. It was the Voulos equivalent of counting to ten. What she did not understand was the flare of dark colour over his hard cheekbones and the momentarily seething look of a male striving not to react to a personal affront.

'I didn't think I was going to need to wear the wretched thing again!' she protested in the hissing silence.

'We'll talk downstairs when you're dressed.' Constantine strode to the door and sent her a slashing glance. 'You owe me an apology for the manner in which you chose to leave my home.'

'I wouldn't hold my breath if I were you.' Rosie tilted her chin. 'I'm not very good at apologising.'

'But you *will* learn,' Constantine spelt out grittily.

Why did he never learn? He was even more stubborn than she was. Grimacing, she slid out of bed. The sparsely furnished bedroom rejoiced in a very old-

fashioned adjoining bathroom. The bath was big enough
to accommodate an entire family. Still in possession of
its Victorian shower attachment, it was the sort of bath
which Maurice would have gone into raptures over, but
unhappily there seemed to be no hot water available.

Her teeth were chattering by the time she had finished
washing. Constantine had used both threadbare towels
and discarded them in a sodden heap on the floor.
Presumably he was also responsible for the lack of hot
water. Even Maurice was better trained as a housemate.
She would have to get dressed to fetch her backpack upstairs and only then would she be able to put on fresh
clothes. However, on her return to the bedroom, Rosie
discovered that she couldn't find a single item of the
clothing which Constantine had unceremoniously ripped
off.

Wrapped in a thin and embarrassingly small wet towel,
Rosie hauled open the bedroom door and shouted at full
volume, 'Constantine!'

Sixty seconds passed. Her toes began to tap on the
dull, unpolished wooden floor. She yelled again. Steps
sounded on the stairs. Rosie smiled and folded her arms.
But it was not Constantine. Dmitri had been sent to deal
with her. Furious, Rosie ducked back behind the door
to conceal her undressed state.

'Mr Voulos is not accustomed to being hailed by a
shout,' Dmitri said in an apologetic whisper voiced in
fluent English from the landing. 'In fact that form of
address puts him in a very bad mood.'

'He's never in anything else,' Rosie grumbled.

'He still feels the loss of Mr Estrada very deeply.'

That quiet, sobering reminder drained Rosie's face of
colour. No, she hadn't made any allowances for the ef-
fects of grief on Constantine's temperament, had she?

'How may I help you, *kiria*?' Dmitri prompted in the
ringing silence.

'It's not important.' Rosie closed the door again and sank down on the edge of the bed.

Since her father's death she had been pretty bad-tempered too, and how many nights had she lain sleepless? Something would happen and she would want to tell Anton about it and then, once more, she would have to come to terms with the fact that he was no longer there to eagerly receive her every confidence and never would be again. After twenty years how much greater that sense of loss must be for Constantine... and surely it was all wrong that they still could not behave like civilised human beings with each other?

A maid knocked on the door and entered, almost staggering under the weight of the garment bags she was carrying. Laying her burden down on a chair, she left the room again. A split second later Constantine strode in with two leather cases.

'Right, obviously you're moving in here... when do I get my clothes back so that I can move out?' Rosie demanded, but after her recent unsettling thoughts her tone was less tart than usual.

'These *are* your clothes,' Constantine responded. 'I bought them between flights on my travels.'

Her fiery head tipped back. 'Why would you buy me clothes?'

'You have nothing appropriate to wear. Consider the new wardrobe a gift.'

Her green eyes glittered. 'That's very generous of you, Constantine... but I would prefer to have my own clothes returned.'

'No. Why do you think I removed them?'

'Removed them... *removed* them? You ripped them off me!'

Constantine dealt her a dark, brooding appraisal, his sensual mouth compressing. 'I find it distasteful that you should wear garments bought by another man.'

'Actually I bought what I was wearing in the cheapest shop I could find in Palma.'

Anger burnished his black eyes. 'You know very well what I am telling you. That dress you wore at the hotel...Anton purchased that, did he not?'

Rosie nodded with a bemused frown.

'So I have made a clean sweep. *Theos*...I can do without the reminder that you were *his* woman first!' Constantine completed in a positive snarl, enraged at being forced to explain his peculiar behaviour.

'Apart from the fact that I am not *any* man's woman—'

'You are mine now.'

'I beg your pardon?' Rosie breathed.

'Anton gave you to me.'

'Say that again,' Rosie invited tremulously, outraged by that particular choice of words.

'And if I am to accept that you are my responsibility I expect you to conform to *my* expectations and respect *my* wishes from now on.'

'I don't conform, Constantine.'

'You will with me.'

'I want my clothes back!' Rosie slammed back at him as she leapt upright, no longer able to stand him towering over her.

He reached for her.

'I hate you...get your lousy hands off me!'

Those same hands framed her wildly flushed cheekbones. Glittering black eyes slashed down into hers in rampant challenge. 'You were clinging to me like a limpet when I woke up, *pethi mou*. I had to give you the pillow to clutch instead.'

'If you weren't so much bigger, I'd knock your teeth down your conceited throat!'

'You see ... you're learning already. A week ago you would have physically attacked me,' Constantine murmured with raw satisfaction.

Rosie shuddered with rage and turbulent confusion. Constantine let both of his hands slowly slide into her bright hair and at the caressing brush of those long brown fingers on her scalp she shivered convulsively, like a woman caught up in a violent storm. He released her with a wolfish smile, dark, measuring eyes scanning her with disturbing intensity. 'You can bite all you like tonight, little rag-doll. I'm very adaptable to new experiences in bed.'

As the door closed, Rosie fell back against the bed for support. Of course he hadn't meant that ... he couldn't possibly be telling her that he expected to make love to her tonight. All she had to do was to say no if he made any advances ... *all*? Hurriedly, she repressed the suspicion that saying no to Constantine might not be that easy.

What on earth had happened to her barely formed desire to begin trying to civilise relations between them? Within thirty seconds he had had her at screaming pitch again. Why the new wardrobe? And why more clothes than even a rich, spoilt socialite could surely wear in the space of two short months? On their wedding day, Constantine had complained because she wasn't wearing one of the snazzy outfits which he had correctly assumed that Anton had bought her ... and *now*?

Now it appeared to be a hanging offence for her to possess a single garment which Anton might have paid for! Her head was aching. It was tension ... pounding, throbbing tension and that awful sense of being horribly out of her depth again.

CHAPTER SEVEN

PERSPIRATION dewed Rosie's short upper lip as she walked the length of the big, dark dining room with its massive carved furniture, tracked every step of the way by Constantine's coolly appreciative appraisal. Was it madness to think that there was a gleam of ownership in that look? Was it even greater madness to consider lunging across the table at him to insist that he *stop* looking at her like that?

'I knew that colour would look stunning against that wonderful hair.'

Rosie flushed, murderously self-conscious in her finery. Expensive or not, it was a plain little green summer dress and she had chosen it in preference to half a dozen more revealing outfits, only to discover that once the fabric was filled with living female flesh it outlined every slim curve with disturbing clarity.

'Why did you bring staff here...surely you're not planning to stay long in a house you described as a ruin?' Rosie prompted tautly as she took a seat opposite him.

'The other wing of the house is uninhabitable but I believe we can manage to exist with the privations in this wing for a few weeks—'

'A few *weeks*?'

'Why not? What could be more conventional than a newly married couple seeking the seclusion of a mountain villa?' Constantine watched her bridle with the indolent cool of a sunbathing big cat.

'Why do you have to keep on reminding me about that stupid wedding ceremony?' Rosie snapped.

113

Disturbing amusement flared in his brilliant dark gaze. 'I think it's time we called a truce.'

'A...truce?' Rosie echoed uncertainly.

Constantine released his breath in a hiss of impatience. 'I had every excuse to be outraged by the terms of Anton's will. Possibly I overreacted but Anton was more dear to me than my own father. It was a great shock to learn that he had another woman in his life.'

'He didn't. How many times do I have to say it? I was *not* his mistress! You were in that house,' Rosie pressed in a tone of frantic appeal. 'You must have noticed that we had separate bedrooms!'

Constantine shifted a broad shoulder in a fluid shrug but his strong face hardened. 'Your sleeping arrangements were of no interest to me.'

'But—'

Constantine slung her a chilling look. 'I have never slept a night through in a woman's bed. Does that mean that I am a celibate?' he traded with sardonic emphasis.

It did not but the information somehow stabbed Rosie like a knife. She veiled her eyes from his but nothing could wipe out a fleeting, distressing image of Constantine sliding out of the lovely Louise's arms in the early hours to head home. 'You're such a cold fish,' she condemned helplessly. 'The minute you've had what you wanted, you take off. You should be ashamed to admit that.'

An arc of faint colour scored Constantine's cheekbones. His mouth clenched hard. 'Sex is an exchange of mutual physical pleasure—'

'Wham-bam, thank you ma'am. No romance, no affection, no feelings. No wonder Anton was mortified by your attitude to women!'

Constantine went white beneath his bronzed skin. *'Christos...'* he ground out raggedly, hanging on to his temper by a hair's breadth.

In similar shock at the attack she had made on him, Rosie dropped her fiery head. But imagine falling in love with a guy like that! she thought. Her mind ran on unstoppably... A cold, unfeeling swine who talked smoothly about exchanging physical satisfaction and who desired no deeper connection in a relationship. Listening to him made her blood curdle in her veins.

'I see nothing wrong in my views.'

'What about love?'

'I have never been in love...' Constantine dealt her a slashing look of driven impatience. 'I don't believe in it. Now, if you were to talk to me of infatuation or lust—'

'No, thanks. I think you've let yourself down enough for one day.' Rosie picked up her knife and fork to embark on the first course of her meal. Somehow she just didn't want to look at Constantine any more. He had *never* been in love? Even with Cinzia Borzone? But then he probably wouldn't recognise the emotion unless it came with a fat price tag attached and was offered via his mobile phone!

Her preoccupied gaze strayed from the elaborately presented dish to the ring lying on the white linen tablecloth. She dropped her cutlery with a noisy clatter, snatched up the Estrada emerald and whispered uncertainly, '*Why* are you giving it back to me?'

'Don't flatter me. I was merely the courier. You left it behind in England.'

'The last time I saw this ring, it was in my jewel case.'

'I think not. Maurice found it on the windowsill in the kitchen.'

Rosie reddened with guilty discomfiture as she threaded the ornate gem back onto her finger. 'I don't remember leaving it there. I honestly did think that I had put it away. I'm sorry I accused you of taking it,' she muttered in a very small voice.

'He also accepted full and complete responsibility for that newspaper article.'

Rosie's chin came up, her wide eyes pained. *'No!'*

Constantine studied her shocked face with cool, dark, incisive eyes. 'You're incredibly naïve in some ways,' he mused. 'You put Maurice in possession of a story worth a great deal of money. He went for the money—'

'I can't believe that...I just can't!'

'He admitted it to me.' Constantine held her distraught gaze steadily. 'I owe you an apology for calling you a cheat.'

Rosie dropped her head again. 'It doesn't matter.'

'It matters to me,' Constantine murmured levelly. 'I misjudged you. But why did you pretend that you *were* responsible?'

Rosie struggled to swallow the thick lump forming in her throat. 'I...I—'

'Every move you make seems to be based on a pathetic need to protect a man who betrayed you without a second's hesitation,' Constantine drawled with derision.

Rosie rose almost clumsily upright. 'I'm not feeling very hungry,' she muttered unsteadily, and walked out of the room as fast as her feet would carry her.

It hurt so very, very much to believe that Maurice could have sold out their friendship for profit. Yes, she had always known that money was important to Maurice and that he was very ambitious, but his business was booming and he was anything but short of ready cash! Peering with tear-filled eyes into a room that seemed to be bustling with people fussing with office equipment, Rosie cannoned blindly into a uniformed maid and then fled out of the open front doors into the sunlight. Even the courtyard wasn't empty, and she raced past the van being industriously unloaded and out into the garden, seeking cover and privacy in the same way that an injured animal seeks darkness.

A convulsive sob was torn from her then. She covered her working face with her spread hands and from behind her came two supporting arms which inexorably turned her round. Gasping, she went rigid, a long shudder of repressed emotion quivering through her.

'Don't be scared, *pethi mou*...it is only me,' Constantine murmured roughly, as if it were the most natural thing in the world that he should attempt to hold her close in a comforting embrace. 'It hurts when people let you down...'

'He's the only man I've ever trusted...apart from Anton,' Rosie framed, fighting a losing battle against the tears pouring down her cheeks.

Constantine drew her hands down from her face but with a sudden jerk Rosie pulled away, turning her narrow back defensively on him.

'How long have you known Maurice?'

'Since I was thirteen... And it was weird,' she whispered thickly in recollection. 'Before I got to know him, I was more scared of him than I was of any of the other boys in the home.'

'What home?'

Rosie loosed a choky laugh. 'When my mother died, my stepfather put me into care.'

'Why?' Constantine shot at her with fierce incomprehension.

'Because I wasn't his. He only found out that Mum was expecting me *after* he married her.'

'Yet he stayed married to her...why didn't he divorce her?' Constantine demanded.

Rosie compressed her lips. Nothing was ever that simple. Tony Waring had been her mother's first serious boyfriend. He had pleaded with her to marry him before she'd gone down to London to find a secretarial job.

When she had returned home and said yes, he had been too overjoyed to question her sudden change of heart. Her mother had told her that bit of the story more than once in an effort to make Rosie understand that her stepfather was entitled to be bitter, that he had been wronged and that it wouldn't be fair to expect him to treat Rosie the same way as he did his own two sons.

'He loved her but he just could never get over her doing that to him,' Rosie muttered tightly. 'They had two kids of their own and he still couldn't forget, so once she was gone there was no way he was going to keep me.'

'What age were you?'

'Nine. I went into a council home and then a lot of short-term foster homes. I kept on running away, so I got a name for being difficult. The place I finally ended up in had some very rough inmates.'

'Including Maurice?'

'He was only there because the authorities had to keep him close to the hospital his mother was in. His sister was fostered but not too many families want to foster teenage boys. I don't want to talk about this...' Rosie started walking away, too upset to be able to understand why she had told Constantine embarrassing, private things that were absolutely none of his business.

'You really love that profiteering ape,' Constantine breathed with savage incredulity. 'And he's a low-life bastard who would rent you out by the hour if he could get away with it!'

Rosie spun round, her tear-wet face appalled. 'How dare you say that?'

'He thrust you at me. He set the two of us up. Did he care what kind of man I was? Or how I might treat you when that story broke?'

'He couldn't have thought—he just couldn't have...' Rosie argued brokenly.

'You say one more word in his defence and I'll fly over to England and rip him apart with my bare hands!' Constantine roared at her in a thunderous, seething fury that shook her so much that she stared wide-eyed. 'And before you ask me why I didn't do that the day before yesterday remind yourself that he knows the *whole* story and not just the tiny part that was published! I have no desire to wake up some day soon to the tale of your sordid affair with Anton!'

Constantine stalked off and then as swiftly turned back again and strode with daunting purpose back across the rough grass. He closed a lean hand over hers. 'You are coming back inside to finish your meal—'

'No.'

'My wife is not going to skulk in the garden and snivel for the entertainment of my staff!'

Rosie gulped. 'Why are you so angry?'

'That is a very stupid question. In fact that may go down in history as the most stupid question I have *ever* been asked!'

Constantine produced an immaculate white handkerchief and dabbed with ruthless but surprising gentleness at her damp cheeks. Rosie studied him with reddened, bemused eyes. 'Oh, *right*,' she muttered, believing she had found the answer to behaviour that was plunging her into ever deeper confusion. 'You don't want the pretend marriage to fall apart this obviously so soon—'

In response, Constantine bent his arrogant dark head and ravished apart her startled lips in a plundering, passionate kiss. Fire leapt into her limp body and blazed through every skin cell with explosive efficiency. Reeling dizzily with the force of her response, Rosie met blazing golden eyes as he lifted his head again.

Screening his gaze, Constantine surveyed her with disturbing calm. 'We'll dine out at the Formentor tonight.

That should give the staff time to get the house into some
sort of order.'

Garbed in a divinely sophisticated evening gown in
glistening pearl-grey, Rosie was surprised to appreciate
just how much she was enjoying herself. The hotel was
fabulous and she had even recognised one or two famous
faces amongst the other diners. But Constantine was undeniably the most gorgeous-looking male present. That
spectacular bone structure, that golden skin and those
incredibly compelling dark, long-lashed eyes...

There wasn't a woman in the place who hadn't looked
at him at least twice and yet amazingly he was feeding
her champagne and flattering *her* with his undivided attention. He hadn't even spared a glance at the arrival of
an only minimally dressed blonde bombshell who had
turned every other male head in the room.

'You're very quiet, *pethi mou*,' Constantine
murmured.

It took a terrifying amount of will-power to drag her
disobedient gaze from him. Angry with herself, her
colour heightened, Rosie watched candlelight twinkle
across the slender platinum wedding band on her finger.
A frown pleated her brow. Earlier that evening, a jeweller
had arrived at Son Fontanal with an extensive selection
of rings and a replacement had been picked. Constantine
had actually laughed about the fact that she had binned
the first ring. Why was he being nice all of a sudden?

'Rosie...what are you thinking about?' He said the
abbreviated version of her name for the very first time
and somehow it sounded so different the way he said it.
That honey-dark drawl made her stupid heart skip a beat.

Studying her champagne glass, Rosie drew in a deep,
steadying breath. 'I was thinking about Maurice,' she
lied, shaken that she had so easily forgotten what had
hurt so much only hours earlier.

'*Theos...*' Constantine breathed with flaring impatience. 'The throwback haunts us!'

Her head tilted back, eyes bright with anger. 'He may not have your education or your status but when I needed him Maurice was always there for me.'

'Only not when your needs conflicted with his avarice.' Lounging fluidly back in his chair, Constantine slung the reminder at her with contempt.

'You can't expect anyone to put you first all the time... even Anton didn't,' Rosie conceded with difficulty. 'But when I most needed Maurice he didn't let me down...' Her voice trailed away and in a nervous movement she drained the champagne in her glass.

'I'm still listening,' Constantine prompted drily.

Her face stiff with strain, Rosie swallowed hard. 'When I was thirteen, two boys forced their way into my room and tried to assault me... Maurice stopped them and because there were two of them he took a hell of a beating doing it.'

Constantine had paled but his gleaming gaze was veiled in the thunderous silence, his sensual mouth twisting. 'Do I start calling him St George instead of the throwback? Maybe you should answer one question before I decide... How long was it before he took with your agreement what the others tried to take by force?'

Rosie flinched as though he had struck her. 'Why...is that how *you* would have behaved?'

Registering her distress, Constantine frowned and abruptly stretched a hand across the table to reach for her tightly coiled fingers. 'Rosie, I—'

In stark rejection of that gesture, Rosie trailed her fingers free and said starkly, 'I reminded him of his kid sister. When he was a child, he had to look after Lorna because their mother was an alcoholic. But after they went into care Lorna was adopted by her foster family and Maurice was left out in the cold. They let them stay

in contact but it wasn't the same. So if you want an
explanation for why he stuck his neck out for me that
night think *clean*—or would that be too much of a challenge for you?'

Tears brightening her eyes, Rosie didn't even look at
him as she thrust her chair back and walked out of the
dining room. He caught up with her in the foyer, a lean
hand curving round her rigid spine and settling on her
waist to still her. 'Rosie—'

'*Constantine!*' a female voice shrilled ecstatically.

Constantine froze and winced as Rosie's head spun
round. The blonde bombshell in the unbelievably tiny
black dress was bearing down on them, full breasts
heaving, voracious blue eyes glittering with satisfaction.
'When did you arrive?' she demanded, literally
wrenching him free of Rosie to plant an intimate and
lingering kiss full on his mouth. 'Doesn't *this* bring back
memories of Monte Carlo, darling?' she moaned
throatily, running caressing hands over any bit of him
she could reach and trying for a place or two that no
lady should aim at in public.

Constantine detached himself with distinct hauteur,
the faintest colour accentuating the hard slant of his
cheekbones as his black eyes skimmed with curious ex-
pectancy to Rosie.

'Justine . . . this is my wife, Rosalie,' he drawled with
supreme self-command.

'Oh, don't mind me,' Rosie said sweetly. 'I'm not the
tiniest bit possessive about you.'

'You've got married? *You*?' Justine looked thunder-
struck and finally took Rosie under her notice. 'To *her*?'
she gasped in stricken incomprehension as she gawped
at Rosie. 'But why?'

'If you get me in the right mood, I even loan him out,'
Rosie imparted with a slanting smile beneath which she
boiled with rage. Then she turned on her heel and stalked

out into the night air. Momentarily her head reeled and she knew that she had drunk a little too much champagne.

But no wonder Constantine hadn't looked at the blonde bombshell falling out of her dress! Been there, done that... and the creep had had the neck to call *her* a tart! Rosie did not flaunt herself half-naked and she would cut off her hands sooner than make such a blatant pass at any man in front of an audience of interested spectators.

Several steps beyond the doors, Constantine reached her and closed a hand over her forearm. '*Christos*...how dare you refer to our marriage and to *me* in such terms?' he gritted rawly.

'Let's get this straight, Constantine...' Rosie stopped dead, her oval face flushed with equal fury. '*We are not married.* Got it? If ever I do get married, I will get married in church and the groom will be someone I at least like and respect. He will not be a hypocritical, insensitive, conceited swine who can't think beyond the level of a one-night stand! So go take a hike!'

'Don't speak to me like that!' Constantine seethed.

'And your taste in women is *pitiful*!' Rosie seethed back, unable to restrain her overwhelming need to pass on that opinion. 'So why waste your time being nice to me all evening? You must have had a far better time in Monte Carlo, *darling* Constantine! You're a womaniser and I wouldn't touch you with a barge-pole!'

'*Theos*...is that a fact?' Constantine roared.

'Yes, that is a fact, *darling*!' Rosie mimicked with vicious pleasure.

A flash of bright light temporarily blinded her and she blinked in bewilderment, straining to focus on a man in a white shirt darting away with a camera. Constantine took advantage of her stasis to grab her with two furiously angry hands and bring his mouth down hotly on hers. *Whoosh*! It felt as if the top of her head was flying off, closely followed by the rest of her startled body taking off into orbit with it. *I lied*, was the last thought she had as her angry fingers knotted fiercely into his thick black hair and held him to her, wanting him, hating him, needing him with a savage passion that was utterly outside her control.

Afterwards, she didn't remember getting into the car. Dmitri had looked suitably grave head-on but from the back seat and through the thick glass separating them Rosie watched his big shoulders give a betraying little quiver and looked hurriedly away again, mortification eating her alive.

'I was offensive and you were justifiably angry but when I followed you out of the dining room I intended to apologise,' Constantine admitted with raw-edged clarity.

'Wow,' Rosie said, but she was still trembling and deep down inside she was a stricken bag of nerves. She had been *jealous*, jealous for the first time in her life! Justine's familiar advances to Constantine had filled her with rage and she had lost her head. Now the paparazzi had a photo of them having a stand-up fight outside the hotel.

'Your behaviour was...' Constantine seemed to be struggling to find the right word in English.

'Appalling,' Rosie slotted in heavily. 'But maybe we should try to look on the bright side of this—'

'*Christos*...you sound like Anton...the roof has fallen in, let us be joyful that the walls still stand!' Constantine grated incredulously. 'What bright side?'

Rosie coiled her trembling hands together. 'If that picture is published, it'll accelerate the break-up, won't it?'

Constantine frowned without comprehension. 'The break-up?'

'When our fake marriage ends. I mean, obviously if we're so badly matched we're at each other's throats within days of the wedding and we've got the publicity to prove it, we shouldn't need to wait a whole two months to split up and go for a divorce,' Rosie pointed out tightly.

'There is a cloud in every silver lining.'

'You've got that the wrong way round.' Suddenly Rosie was feeling horribly depressed and wondering if it was that awful loss of temper which was responsible or the decided awareness that she definitely did not hate Constantine the way she had believed she did. What she hated and feared was the extraordinary power he had over her emotions.

'Have I?'

A strained silence stretched.

'When I asked how long it was before you became intimately involved with Maurice, I spoke without thought. I was not being as insensitive as I may have sounded,' Constantine framed in a roughened undertone. 'I was very disturbed to learn that you had endured a vicious assault at that age but I do not see Maurice as your saviour beyond that one gallant act...in fact I now see him as a yob who took advantage of your hero-worship and gratitude.'

From throwback to yob. Had Maurice risen from rock-bottom in Constantine's estimation? It was hard to tell. But she herself had definitely sunk and shrunk in stature. Constantine no longer talked as if he thought she was the more dominant partner in the relationship. Now she sounded like a poor little victim.

'I am not intimately involved with Maurice,' Rosie muttered, biting hard at her lower lip.

'Not now, not any longer,' Constantine stated with grim emphasis, his strong jawline clenching as he shot her a sardonic glance. 'And when we go our separate ways, if I have anything to do with it, you will not be crawling back to him! He's a bad influence on you.'

'I'm twenty, not ten, Constantine.'

'But you still tell as many lies as a child.' As the car drew to a halt in the courtyard at Son Fontanal, Constantine murmured drily, 'Do you really think I could believe that you haven't slept with *either* of the men you were living with? Or that Anton forced me to marry you over anything less than his honest belief that you were expecting his child?'

'Don't you dare call me a liar!' Springing out of the limo, Rosie stalked indoors.

'I console myself with one reflection,' Constantine drawled as he drew level with her in the stone-flagged hall. 'Had you been pregnant by Anton or indeed *had* there been a blood-tie between you—' a derisive laugh expressed his opinion of that possibility '—I would have been trapped in this marriage for the rest of my days.'

Disbelief halted Rosie in her tracks. 'That's...that's a crazy thing to say.'

'Crazy?' His winged brows drew together in genuine astonishment at the charge, his black eyes frowning. 'In either of those circumstances it would have been a matter of honour that I should fully accept the obligation he laid upon me.'

'But that's outrageous...' Rosie condemned unevenly.

'To you, perhaps,' Constantine conceded wryly. 'But Anton brought me up and I had enormous respect for him. I owe him a great deal. He had a very strong sense of duty towards his family. That kind of loyalty *should* take precedence over personal feelings.'

A jerky little laugh fell from Rosie's dry lips as she found herself blindly studying her feet. Suddenly she was very grateful that she had not repeated her claim that she was Anton's daughter. She had a vision of Constantine hog-roped and tied to her out of respect for her father's last wishes. 'A matter of honour', he called it. She winced at the demeaning concept but a tinge of curiosity remained.

'Are you actually saying that you would have married a stranger and stayed married to her just because that was what Anton asked you to do?' she prompted.

'I have married a stranger... only you become more familiar and yet more strange with every minute I spend in your company,' Constantine confessed with a sudden fierceness that made her shiver. 'I do not understand you... and I will not be satisfied until I do!'

Rosie moved away a step. She wasn't even looking at him. Already she had learnt that defence but it wasn't working now. The darkly passionate rasp of his voice made her feel all hot and sort of quivery and even a foot from him she knew she was still too close for safety.

'Look at me...' Constantine invited softly.

Rosie was in retreat. 'I think I—'

'I am not a womaniser.'

'If you say so.'

'I had a brief and foolish affair with Justine when I was only twenty-one.'

'Gosh... you must have made some impression!' Accidentally meeting his intent golden eyes, Rosie became alarmingly short of breath. Without fully appreciating what she was doing, she started up the staircase backwards.

'My wealth made the deepest impression.' Constantine spread eloquent and dismissive hands as he strolled towards her with the fluid prowl of a lion tracking a nervous prey. 'Yet it appears to mean little to you. That is a new experience for me and a most surprising response from you.'

'Really?' Rosie's strained query wobbled as she flipped up two whole steps at once, tightly gripping the worn balustrade for support. 'Why surprising?'

'Had you been as avaricious as I believed, you would have played on the attraction between us. You would have been eager to share my bed in the expectation of profiting from that intimacy,' Constantine responded with a slow, devastating smile. 'But while the flesh was weak the will was stronger still and you were not tempted by the thought of what surrender might bring you.'

'Constantine,' Rosie said slightly shrilly, still heading up and back but utterly powerless to disengage her mesmerised gaze from the dark lure of his. 'Hasn't it occurred to you that I might be the kind of devious woman who thinks that you could thrive on a challenge?'

'But you know that truth as if you were *born* knowing it, *pethi mou*,' Constantine savoured with disconcerting amusement, raking her with burnished eyes of appreciative gold. 'Why else would you fight with me?'

'Because...because...' Rosie fumbled wildly for a reason as she reached the landing and tried to step up. She might have lost her balance had Constantine not reached out and swiftly steadied her with strong hands. 'Because you irritate the hell out of me...that's why I fight with you!' she managed in a surge of frantic rebellion.

'You fight with me,' Constantine traded in a husky growl of disagreement, 'to hold me at bay. But you've used that ploy once too often, and I may have been a slow learner but, believe me, when I catch on I'm faster than the speed of light and from now on every time you shout at me I will cover your mouth with mine.'

'It won't work...I'm naturally argumentative!' Rosie asserted even more tautly.

Golden fire in his molten appraisal, Constantine swept her up into his arms to carry her into the bedroom. '*Christos*...of course it will work. And once we have made love, once you have lain in my arms and tasted the pleasure we can share, you will never mention the throwback again. I may not be perfect but I'm way beyond him in the reliability stakes.'

Rosie looked up at him, her heart racing so fast, it thundered in her ears. 'We c-can't do this,' she stammered.

'We can...let me show you *how*,' Constantine groaned achingly against the corner of her mouth, his breath fanning her cheek. A hunger she couldn't fight shot through her with the shattering shock effect of a lightning bolt and, reacting on pure instinct to the almost pleading quality of that deep, dark drawl, she turned her mouth under his...and burned.

CHAPTER EIGHT

ROSIE surfaced from that kiss to find herself on the bed. Her dress started falling off as she pulled herself up on one elbow and she snatched at the wildly dipping neckline which was threatening to expose her breasts. A vaguely exploring hand discovered the reason for that lack of suspension. Her zip was down. In a daze she focused on Constantine.

Already he was half-undressed and he was watching her intently, a curious smile playing about his wide, wickedly sensual mouth. 'Why do you act so shy? Do you only make love in the dark?'

A flush of pink ran up beneath her skin. Meeting those brilliant black eyes, she found it was so incredibly hard to breathe or to think but oh, so easy to *feel* the pulse of throbbing excitement that beat in tune with her racing heart. Do I want to do this? Rosie asked herself in sudden turmoil. Oh, yes. Should I? *Definitely not.* Hitching her dress with an unsteady hand, she snaked a foot slowly towards the edge of the bed.

Constantine strolled forward with immense calm and tugged her shoes off. His mobile phone buzzed. He tensed. Rosie watched him expectantly as he reached for it. The buzz stopped. 'What are you doing?' she whispered.

'Switching it off—'

'But it might be an important call!'

Beneath Rosie's deeply shaken gaze, Constantine shrugged. 'It can wait until morning, *pethi mou.*'

A whole night in Constantine's arms, Rosie found herself savouring, and then she stopped herself dead. There was no such thing as a whole night with Constantine. As soon as he had satisfied his lust, he would be off to sleep elsewhere. *His lust*. Dear heaven, how could she even be thinking of making love with him? That anguished question had little hope of a rational answer when she discovered that she could think of nothing else.

'You're very nervous,' Constantine murmured with a frown as he slid out of his well-cut trousers.

'I am not nervous,' Rosie stated with a shrill and desperate stab at dignity as she finally worked up sufficient will-power to scramble off the bed, hotly flushed and contorting herself to struggle with her zip. 'But I'm afraid you can't buy me with dinner and a new wardrobe... or even a reasonable pretence of being human for five minutes—'

Constantine intercepted her, confident hands closing over her rigid shoulders. 'You don't have to be scared of me. I'm not rough in bed,' he told her huskily. 'Not unless you want me to be...'

Finding herself backed up against the bed, Rosie stammered. 'C-Constantine...'

'Your heart is going crazy, *pethi mou*.'

In the act of clamping a guilty hand to the offending organ, Rosie discovered that Constantine had got there first. A warm palm curved against the pouting swell of her breast and she trembled at that light yet possessive touch, her eyes involuntarily closing on a tide of sexual awareness so powerful that her legs threatened to buckle beneath her. *'Don't!'* she gasped strickenly.

But he slowly slid the straps of her dress all the way down her arms and simultaneously pressed his mouth to the precise spot where a pulse was flickering wildly at the base of her throat. A faint moan escaped Rosie as he simply lifted her out of her dress and settled her back on the bed again.

'I'll be very gentle,' Constantine promised thickly, with emphasis.

Her lashes flew up to encounter molten gold enquiry. One look and her bones felt as if they were melting beneath her skin. He came down beside her, lithe and dark and naked, and her heart gave a reactive lurch as she ran wondering, curious eyes over his impressive, powerful length. Her startled eyes widened at the bold, hard thrust of his manhood and she ran out of breath all at once, hot colour and alarm seizing her in a twin attack as, curiosity more than satisfied, she made an entirely instinctive move to escape again.

Constantine rolled over so fast to prevent that that she found herself trapped under him instead, a position that made her even more overpoweringly aware of what she had decided she ought to avoid. *'Theos...'* he grated as he stared down into her anxious, evasive eyes. 'I wish I had smashed Maurice's face in... what the hell did he *do* to you in bed?'

'Nothing!'

'I am not going to hurt you...' Constantine ran a caressing finger along the tense compression of her soft, full mouth, brilliant golden eyes shimmering over her, mesmerically sentencing her to stillness. 'I bet he's never heard of foreplay... Even if it takes me all night to prove it, I swear you will enjoy every moment with me, *pethi mou.*' With the tip of his finger he pressed apart her lips and gently probed the moist cavern within while she stared up at him, lost in those compelling eyes of his, and her lips curved round that finger, laving it with her tongue.

Constantine smiled. Rosie's heart flipped. He withdrew his finger, dropped his dark head and traced the fullness of her lower lip with the teasing tip of his tongue. She wanted him to kiss her. It was an instantaneous need and she shifted beneath him, all of a quiver with helpless impatience, her body taut with sudden screaming tension. Her hands flew up of their own volition and her fingers sank into his black hair to try and drag him down to her by force.

With a husky laugh, Constantine resisted her urging and instead let his tongue dip between her readily parted lips. 'Foreplay,' he whispered provocatively.

But, in the grip of hunger, Rosie wasn't that easily quelled. She reached up until she found his sensual mouth for herself, forcing the pace by wrenching him down to her, not satisfied until he kissed her long and hard and then learning that she still wasn't satisfied. But he was ahead of her then, shifting down her trembling length and letting knowing fingers glance over her swelling breasts and linger like the kiss of fire on the straining thrust of her taut nipples.

All the breath left her lungs in a strangled moan of tortured pleasure. Gazing down at her, Constantine made a husky soothing sound deep in his throat. It was incredibly sexy. He bent his head, long fingers pressing the pouting mounds together, and licked the rosy peaks gently and then more rapidly until her back arched on a long, sighing gasp. As he toyed with those achingly sensitive buds, Rosie whimpered and jerked, flames of tormented excitement building in an uncontrollable surge. Her hands skimmed with wild indecision over every part of him she could reach, tangling in his hair, smoothing over his blunt cheekbones, clutching at the smooth, muscular expanse of his shoulders.

Constantine rolled over, carrying her with him so that she was lying on top of him, and plundered her soft mouth with a force of passion that splintered through her squirming body at storm force. Meshing a hand into her mane of hair, he tugged her head up to look at her with burning golden eyes. 'Would you like five minutes to cool down?' he asked thickly.

'Cool down?' Rosie echoed breathlessly as if he were talking in a foreign language, the throbbing tips of her breasts grazed by the rough black curls on his chest, making her eyes slide shut again on a silent shiver of utterly boneless pleasure. She moved so that she could rub herself against him again and moaned.

A thick flood of Greek was wrenched from Constantine, his long, hard frame shuddering beneath hers in enforced response. Hard hands closed round her hips and dragged her up his extended length, parting her thighs so that she straddled him. 'I need to cool down...no, I *need*—' And he closed his mouth hungrily over a rosy nipple, jolting her with such a shock of intense sensation that she cried out, her head falling back.

He splayed long fingers over the ripe curve of her behind to settle her exactly where he wanted her and rock her back and forth over the velvet-smooth thrust of his arousal with an earthy groan of satisfaction. Rosie moaned in shivering, startled reaction to that new source of excitement, out of control and irretrievably lost in the violent surge of pleasure he was giving her. She burned and ached and craved more with a hunger that threatened to tear her apart.

'*Please...*' she gasped.

Constantine flipped her back onto the mattress and kissed her again, his tongue delving in electrifying imitation of an infinitely more invasive possession. At the same time he ran a knowing hand down the straining slender expanse of her inner thigh, making every tiny muscle in her entire body jerk, and fleetingly skimmed the moist, throbbing centre of her.

'You feel like hot satin,' he groaned against her swollen mouth.

Touched where she had never been touched before, Rosie was incapable of a vocal response. Her whole being was centred on the tormenting exploration of those skilful fingers. She wanted to thrash about and he wouldn't let her. Her heart slammed like a hammer against her breastbone as she sobbed for breath, driving to such a wild pitch of excitement that she was convinced she was being deliberately tortured.

And then, at the height of that teeth-clenching, agonising pleasure, Constantine pulled her under him and plunged into her with the ravishing force of an invading army. Rosie let out a yelp of pain that would have woken the dead and then sank her teeth vengefully into a hard, muscular shoulder. He cursed and flinched into sudden stillness. As the level of agony subsided to a dulled but still perceptible throb, Rosie unclenched her teeth and looked up at him accusingly.

'*Theos*...' Constantine rasped, black eyes expressively awash with guilty, angry bewilderment as he snatched in a ragged breath. 'I'm sorry...you excited me so much, I lost control.'

Incredibly touched by the look of bemusement in those magnetic dark eyes, Rosie's tension gave. 'I—'

His dark, tousled head swooped down, the tender, seductive caress of his mouth feathering against hers in silken persuasion of the cruellest kind. 'But you feel like heaven on earth,' he confided with a sinuous, slow and infinitesimal shift of his hips that sent a rise of reawakened pleasure travelling through her startled body. 'Trust me, *pethi mou*...'

Rosie melted like frost in sunlight, heat surging back in a stabbing little surge of excitement. The next time he moved she was waiting for that feeling and a second after that she was shocked to realise that she was desperately craving more of that astonishingly sensual sensation which sent every pulse racing.

'OK?' Constantine husked.

OK? It was more than OK, it was... it was glorious and so deeply intimate that she felt possessed. Squeezing her eyes shut, Rosie felt the excitement rocket almost terrifyingly fast until all she could do was gasp and cling in abandoned surrender to the hungry, diving stroke of him inside her. And then, before she could even grasp what was happening to her, the heat mushroomed and stars exploded in a multicoloured frenzy behind her eyelids. As he shuddered above her in the grip of his own climax, the tidal wave of extraordinary pleasure still rocking her was mindless in its intensity.

She didn't want Constantine to move and disturb the incredible sense of peace and happiness filling her. And he was inextricably bound up with those feelings, she registered in confusion, instinctively loving the heat and weight of him and the achingly familiar scent of his damp skin.

He lifted his dark head and stared down at her with stunning intensity. Rosie was held fast by that scrutiny and the raw tension now tautening his muscles but his black eyes were utterly unreadable. His mouth twisted. 'You felt like a virgin.' He vented a harsh, almost bitter laugh. 'Or how I *imagine* a virgin would feel! *Christo*, what would I know about that?'

Releasing her from his weight with startling abruptness, Constantine sprang off the bed. 'I need a shower.'

'Constantine...?' Rosie whispered shakily.

'I am sorry I hurt you,' Constantine breathed roughly on the threshold of the bathroom without turning round to look at her again. 'But right now I don't feel good about this development.'

In a shock made raw by a crawling sense of humiliation, Rosie lay listening to the shower running. Constantine regretted the 'development'. Sexual hunger satisfied, Constantine couldn't escape the scene of the crime quickly enough. A great lump closed over Rosie's throat and her eyes stung and burned. She could have stopped him; she could have said no. But she had stupidly indulged herself, indulged him and refused to face up to what she was doing. Yet in her worst imaginings she could not have expected so devastating and immediate a rejection of their intimacy...or the feeling that she was being ripped slowly in two by the strength of her own turbulent emotions.

Constantine emerged from the bathroom again. He banged through every piece of furniture in the room. Curiosity finally drove Rosie's head up. Light glimmered over the long, golden sweep of his back. He was pulling on a pair of jeans, electric tension sizzling like wildfire from every jerky, impatient movement. Fascinated against her will, Rosie stared.

'I'm going out,' Constantine gritted over one brown shoulder.

'Be my guest,' Rosie managed, turning away again and feeling more alone than she had ever felt in her life before. She had felt she knew Constantine but now she knew that she didn't know him at all. She didn't know why he was behaving as he was. She didn't know what was on his mind. Self-loathing boiled through her slender frame. Well, that was what you got when you went to bed with a stranger.

After lying awake for hours, Rosie finally slid into an exhausted sleep around dawn. Shortly after nine, voices below her window woke her up. Workmen were assembling to repair the roof. She had a shower, made unimpressed use of the extravagant number of luxurious new towels available, and while she wondered where Constantine had slept she despised herself for caring.

Downstairs she passed by a closed door beyond which she heard Constantine and a ringing phone. Her strained mouth compressed as a maid directed her into the dining room. Breakfast was served but Rosie had little appetite. She was finishing her coffee when Carmina appeared, beaming behind a huge bouquet of flowers.

'Forgive me,' it said on the card.

Two high spots of colour flared over Rosie's taut cheekbones. Forgive him? Not if he crawled and begged for a hundred years! Her teeth gritted. 'Get her some flowers,' he had probably said to Dmitri. Oh, what a big effort Constantine had made! Why? He was stuck up a mountain, supposedly on his honeymoon, and sexually available women were thinner than hens' teeth on the ground. The threat of celibacy undoubtedly struck horror into his oversexed bones. Had Constantine now decided that he had been too hasty in regretting their intimacy?

Rosie thrust wide the door of the room being used as an office. As an entrance it failed. Everyone was too busy to notice her. A svelte brunette in her thirties was taking notes while standing up. Constantine was dictating in bursts of low-pitched Greek, while simultaneously conducting a conversation on the phone. A young man was seated, muttering over a computer terminal, while another was ripping several feet of paper out of a fax machine.

Rosie crossed the room to the electric shredder, hit the button and started stuffing flowers into the metal jaws. The shredder chewed up the first few inches of the floral sacrifice, wedged shut on the stalks and cut out with a complaining beep of warning. Silence slowly spread and Rosie spun round.

Constantine had lowered his phone. She saw only him, raging green eyes connecting with glittering black as he sprang upright. Sheathed in a lightweight suit in pale grey, he looked devastatingly handsome. As their companions melted out of the room without being asked, Rosie sucked in a deep breath, found it insufficient to cool her temper and battered the remaining blooms in seething frustration against the inanimate shredder before flinging them to the floor in a violent gesture of contempt.

'You unbelievable creep! How *dare* you give me flowers?'

'Last night shouldn't have happened,' Constantine gritted between clenched teeth, brilliant black eyes unflinching. 'But what is done is done.'

Disconcerted by that initial statement, Rosie paled, and even though she knew she ought to agree with the sentiment expressed she was attacked by an amount of pain that tensed every muscle in her slender body. Her lashes dipped to conceal her confusion. 'You were determined to get me into bed,' she condemned.

'*Theos* ... given the overwhelming attraction between us, that conclusion was inevitable! But I'm not very proud that last night I wasn't able to keep my hands off my guardian's mistress,' Constantine stated with fierce candour.

Belated comprehension sank in on Rosie, making her marvel at her lack of perception. Once again, Constantine's firm belief that she had had an affair with Anton had made its prejudice felt ... and *how*, she reflected painfully, recalling the bitter force of his rejection only hours earlier. But with understanding came an odd sense of relief and then a rise of stark frustration. Her chin came up, green eyes flashing a direct challenge. 'How many times do I have to tell you that Anton and I were not lovers?'

Shimmering dark golden eyes collided ferociously fast with hers. Constantine expelled his breath in a driven hiss. 'There's a fool born every minute but I'm not one of them.'

She could go and drag in Carmina and ask her to show that photograph and repeat what Anton had told her, but how embarrassing that would be for all of them ... and *then* what? Even if she actually managed to convince Constantine that she was Anton's daughter, where did they go from there? She might want to clear her name but she couldn't forget what Constantine had admitted with such impressive conviction the night before.

If he knew who she *really* was, would he start thinking of her as some sort of ghastly obligation and out of respect for Anton feel forced to change his behaviour accordingly? She cringed from that idea. At least on these terms they met on level ground. The time would certainly come when she would try to prove her identity but that time was not now, when she couldn't bear to think that owning up to being Anton's illegitimate child might make Constantine pity her.

Staring into those scorching dark eyes, Rosie felt her heart lurch and her mouth run dry. Constantine gazed back at her in the pounding, pulsing silence. Without warning it was incredibly difficult to breathe. Shock reeled over her because this time she couldn't even pretend that she didn't know what was happening to her.

'You told Anton that you were pregnant,' Constantine contended in a ragged, dark growl as he drew inexorably closer. 'It was a cheap trick but that is why he demanded that I marry you.'

'I don't play cheap tricks,' Rosie told him breathlessly, struggling to hang on to her wits as her skin heated and her breasts swelled into throbbing sensitivity. She pressed a betraying hand to the pulse flickering a crazy beat at her collarbone.

'*Christos* ... you play me like a witch casting a spell!'
Constantine countered with sudden glancing rawness. 'I
want you even more now than I wanted you last
night—'

'Tough,' Rosie said with tremulous bite, a quiver of
deep overpowering longing sheeting over her with the
efficacy of a mind-blowing drug, leaving her more dizzy
and disorientated than ever. Her dazed green eyes clung
to his hard, dark face in a tormented craving that cut
like glass through her pride and slashed it to ribbons.

In response, Constantine reached out, curved his
fingers firmly over her stiff shoulders and pulled her
across the floor into his arms. And since that was where
every inch of her wanted to be she couldn't fight. He
crushed her to him in a shatteringly sexual embrace, a
powerful hand pressing her into intimate contact with
the bold, hard thrust of his arousal. Rosie shivered violently, her legs turning hollow. He took her mouth with
hot, hard hunger and the heat of desire blanked out every
thought. She clutched at his broad shoulders, knit frantic
fingers into his thick black hair and feverishly kissed
him back.

He sank down into his swivel chair with her on top
of him, lean hands roving beneath her loose T-shirt,
skimming over the smooth, taut skin of her ribcage in
search of the pouting mounds above. Encountering her
bra, he groaned with frustration against her reddened
mouth, released the fastening with dexterity and spread
both hands possessively over her bared breasts. Fierce
sensation engulfed her in a wild tide of shuddering response. If she had been standing up, she would have
fallen down.

Meshing a hand into the tumble of her hair,
Constantine held her back from him, his breath coming
in tortured bursts. The phone was ringing off the hook,
the fax still noisily spewing paper. A flicker of discon-

certion drew his winged ebony brows together.
Momentarily he closed his eyes as if he was fighting for
control, a muscle pulling taut at the corner of his sensual
mouth. His thumb rubbed over an achingly erect pink
nipple and Rosie trembled and gasped as if she were in
a force-ten-gale, bowing her head over his, resting her
forehead in his luxuriant hair, torn apart and weak as
water with need.

'You are driving me off the edge, *pethi mou*,' Constantine confided with ragged bite. 'Possibly a working
honeymoon was not one of my brighter ideas.' Suddenly
he stood up, both arms anchored around her, and set
her down on the edge of the desk, sending papers flying
with a decisive sweep of one arrogant brown hand. 'But
then if I want to make love to my wife in the middle of
the day that is *my* business.'

Rosie's lashes fluttered. 'I'm not your...' she began,
yet her voice trailed away again, wiped out by the change
she'd discovered within herself, the sea change that had
crept up on her without her noticing. *His wife,* she savoured in a sudden stark surge of possessiveness that
shook her.

Tugging the wide-necked T-shirt down her arms to
entrap her and then slowly extracting her hands,
Constantine delved his tongue between her parted lips
with a growl of immense satisfaction. The hunger he
could heighten with just one more kiss blazed a fiery
trail that plunged her into quivering sensual oblivion.
He skimmed caressing fingers over the straining pink
buds of her nipples, making her burn and shift and moan
with pleasure beneath his mouth, and then he was
pressing her back, his hands skimming up her thighs to
drag her cotton skirt down out of his path as he pulled
her to him.

Clenched by an excitement that made breathing a
torment to her struggling lungs, Rosie focused on him

with wondering eyes, her racing heart threatening to arrest as she drowned in the passionate intensity of his gaze. Utterly entrapped, she arched her spine like a willing sacrifice.

'You make me *ache* . . .' His deep, dark drawl was ragged with arousal as he lowered his mouth to her pouting breasts. 'I want to be inside you so badly, I'm shaking, *pethi mou*.'

The hot pleasure took her by violent storm, strangled moans torn from deep in her throat as he worked his way slowly down her quivering length, and by the time he reached the tensing, jerking concavity of her stomach Rosie was just a mass of melting, gasping nerve-endings, only managing to stay on the desk because he had her pinned there. He was torturing her and she couldn't bear it. He hooked his fingers into the waistband of her high-cut cotton panties and she was on the very brink of exploding with the sheer force of her anticipation when, without the smallest warning, Constantine froze, grabbed up her T-shirt and flung it across her. Her startled eyes flew wide.

Constantine strode towards the opening door at the same time as a thunderous crash of smashing china and rattling metal sounded in the hall outside.

In shock, Rosie jumped a foot in the air. Other noises which she had tuned out swam back into her awareness. The phone was still ringing, the fax still buzzing. She blinked in frantic bemusement. Only one item of clothing stood between her and complete nudity, she registered strickenly. In broad daylight, she was spread across Constantine's desk like a brazen trollop. Oh, dear heaven . . .

Constantine snapped the door softly shut again. 'One of the maids was bringing in coffee. Dmitri intercepted her. He gave her such a fright she dropped the tray. I haven't done anything like this since I was a teenager,' he murmured with sudden rueful amusement.

Rosie refused to look at him. 'Go away!' she said shakily.

'Why?'

She was burning alive in an agony of mortification. 'Get out of here while I get my clothes on!'

'Don't you think that would be just a little absurd in the circumstances?'

'Bloody hell...can you never do *anything* I ask you to do?' Her strained voice cracked on the demand. 'Do you always have to argue about it?'

The door closed with a definitive thud.

Pale as milk, Rosie shot off the desk like a shoplifter caught red-handed in the glare of spotlights. In a mad rush she fumbled clumsily for her bra and her skirt and then crawled about the floor until she finally located a missing canvas pump lying under a chair. As she dressed, tears drenching her distraught eyes, she studied the open window, and then, in sudden decision, pressed it wider to facilitate her exit. It was the work of a moment to hoist herself over the sill and out into the fresh air, thereby cravenly avoiding any immediate further contact with Constantine. Before she dealt with Constantine, she conceded painfully, she needed to deal with what was happening inside her own head.

As she clambered over the stack of roof tiles in her path and worked her way round a ladder, she heard a car coming up the drive. It was a bright yellow four-wheel drive. Drawing the brash vehicle to a halt, the driver vaulted out, blond mane gleaming in the sunshine as he looked curiously around himself. Rosie froze.

'Maurice?' she whispered shakily, and then she shrieked, *'Maurice!'* and closed the distance between them in ten seconds flat to fling herself at him with a strangled sob of welcome.

CHAPTER NINE

ENVELOPING Rosie in a bear hug, Maurice scanned her damp-eyed pallor beneath her wildly tousled hair, an anxious frown in his bright blue eyes. 'You look bloody awful...what's been going on?' he demanded.

'Let's go for a drive!' Pulling free of him, Rosie dived into the passenger seat of the four-wheel drive and looked at him expectantly. 'What are you waiting for?'

'Constantine.' Maurice mimicked the soundtrack from *Jaws*.

'Oh, stop being funny!' Rosie cried as she cast hunted glances in all directions, her nerves shot to hell by an absolute terror of Constantine appearing and dragging her back out of the car. 'I think I'm in love with him!'

There it was, *said*, out in the open, Rosie's worst nightmare come true, and Maurice didn't even have the decency to look surprised.

'What on earth are you doing over here?' she asked belatedly.

Maurice swung the brightly coloured vehicle into an unhurried U-turn. 'I've been promising myself a holiday for a long time. The minute you said you were in Majorca, I saw sun and sand and I realised where you had to be heading. From there it was only a matter of studying the map.'

While he drove down the steep mountain road at the crawling speed of someone terrified of heights, easing round every zigzag bend with an agonised death-grip on the steering wheel, Rosie thought feverishly about

Constantine until her head spun and pounded with tension.

Bang! He had stolen her tranquillity and her security. And what had he given her in return? A hideous sense of inadequacy and self-loathing and a temper as unreliable as an active volcano. If threatened by Constantine, *shout*. Only last night he had been telling her that she argued with him to hold him at bay! He had seen inside her and understood something she hadn't understood herself and that was terrifying.

The minute she had found herself holding fire on protesting her identity, the minute that she had found herself wishing that their marriage were a real marriage, she should have known that she was in love with him. But all Constantine had ever wanted from her was sex. She found him irresistible, he found her... available. If that tabloid hadn't exposed their secret wedding, Constantine would've walked away from her that morning without a backward glance.

'Aren't you even curious about that newspaper article?' Maurice prompted between grinding teeth of strain. 'Or didn't Constantine tell you that I took the blame for that? It's true, it *was* my fault. I shot my mouth off to my sister—'

'Lorna?' Dredged from her introspection, Rosie's head spun round.

'She used to see this bloke, Mitch, in the pub. He was a reporter on the local paper. Apparently, she'd been trying to get off with him for ages,' Maurice explained grimly. 'So she spouted the story to try and impress him with the idea that she had interesting connections, invited him back to her flat for coffee and let him borrow that photo she took of you.'

Only then did Rosie recall that the day she and Maurice had moved into the cottage it had been his sister wielding the camera. Lorna had given *her* a souvenir copy of that photograph.

'And that was the last she saw of him. Mitch swopped the scoop for a job on a London tabloid. It's a lucky thing that I only told Lorna you were marrying Constantine and nothing else. She thinks you met him down in London,' Maurice proffered heavily. 'If she'd known about Anton or the will, that slimy reporter would've got the whole damned lot out of her!'

Rosie sighed. 'You lied to protect her.'

'Constantine is a very confrontational bloke. In fact, he comes out of nowhere like a rocket attack,' Maurice groaned, staring fixedly into the driving mirror.

Rosie stiffened, dismayed to discover words in defence of Constantine brimming to her lips and hurriedly swallowing them back. 'I'm probably just infatuated with him. I'll get over it,' she swore, striving to save face on the subject of a relationship that had no future whatsoever.

'I hope so. Only a maniac with no respect for human life would sit on my bumper on a road as dangerous as this!' Sweat was breaking out on Maurice's brow.

'You mean...?' Rosie's head whipped round at the exact same moment as a low-slung scarlet sports car flashed past them at speed on the brow of the bend and screeched to a tyre-squealing halt.

Panicked by the manoeuvre, Maurice hit the brakes of the four-wheel drive in an emergency stop. Constantine sprang fluidly out of the sports car and strode back towards them.

'He raced cars for a while when he was a teenager,' Rosie explained shakily. 'Thespina persuaded him to give it up.' He took up women instead, she completed inwardly.

'He's walking inches from the edge of a thousand-foot drop without looking where he's going!' Maurice gritted, his appalled gaze glued to the sight.

'Can't you drive on past or something?'

'Are you as crazy as he is?' Maurice demanded in a defensive burst of incredulity. 'I'd need a death wish to try and outrun a Ferrari on this road!'

Constantine stilled three feet from the car and removed his sunglasses, sliding them into the pocket of his exquisitely tailored jacket. Ice-cold black eyes dug into Rosie and she shivered, intimidated more by that chilling, silent menace than she would have been by rage.

Maurice skimmed a rueful glance between the two of them and slowly shook his head. 'Get out of the car, Rosie,' he murmured flatly. 'I'm only a hero on level ground...and, aside of that, Constantine *is* your husband.'

Shock made Rosie's generous mouth fall inelegantly wide.

'Unless, of course, you were about to tell me that he knocks you about...' Maurice dealt her a doubtful but enquiring glance.

A terrible desire to lie assailed Rosie and then she clashed with the raw outrage in Constantine's fulminating stare and shrank with shame. 'But you can't just—'

'I'm sorry, but I'm not taking sides.' With an air of decided finality, Maurice hit the release button on her seat belt.

'How wise,' Constantine purred like the predator he was as he strolled round the bonnet.

'I'll be in touch,' Maurice sighed.

Disdaining the use of the door, Constantine lifted Rosie out of the passenger seat with two powerful hands. 'I can walk,' she snapped, her burning face a picture of temper and mortification. 'Put me down, for heaven's sake!'

In intimidating silence and paying no heed whatsoever to her fevered protests, Constantine strode back down the road and settled her into the Ferrari.

'How dare you treat me like that?' Rosie gasped as he swung in beside her.

'What did you expect... applause for making a fool of yourself?'

'And what's that supposed to mean?'

'Conscience might have brought Maurice over here to check up on you but he wasn't prepared to force the issue with me. Clearly you were telling the truth when you said that you weren't lovers... but the absence of the sexual element wasn't for want of trying on your part, was it?' Constantine slashed her a look of biting derision. 'It is obvious to me that you settled for friendship only because *he* wasn't interested in anything else.'

'That's nonsense...' Rosie began heatedly.

'And then you threw yourself at Anton because you needed to prove to yourself that you were capable of attracting other men! Or was the affair with Anton and the move to London planned as a desperate last-ditch attempt to make Maurice jealous and sit up and take notice of you?'

'Don't be ridiculous... I'm not in love with Maurice.'

'You certainly weren't in love with Anton. But then no doubt he was a father figure,' Constantine responded with sardonic bite.

Rosie froze, her anger decimated by pain. 'That's exactly what he was,' she mumbled.

'And within minutes of that memorial service you weren't lusting after any ghost!'

Rosie reddened fiercely at that earthy reminder of the way Constantine had affected her that day. 'Don't you have any decency?'

The powerful car shot to a halt in the courtyard. Constantine killed the engine and turned his head to look at her, black eyes as hard as jet in his vibrantly handsome face. 'It took a hike when you took off in a tantrum with Maurice. He's your security blanket and I think you're old enough to do without him. Times have changed and don't try to tell me differently, *pethi mou*. It's me that you want now...'

Always and for ever, she thought fearfully, clenched by a bone-deep sense of her own vulnerability. She wanted much more than she had any hope of achieving.

Constantine lifted a lean hand and caught a colourful handful of corkscrew curls gently between his fingers. He tipped her troubled face up to the onslaught of his starkly assessing gaze. 'And I want you,' he completed with lethal brevity. 'So what's the problem? As I see it, it's a simple and perfectly straightforward relationship.'

Rosie snatched in a sustaining breath, almost drowning in the evocative scent of him so close, a whole chain of little reactions making her head swim and her body quiver. 'But then you only think with your hormones—'

'*Theos*, I can't think with anything else around you,' Constantine admitted thickly, unconcerned by her censure.

Rosie struggled to suppress a shiver of excitement. Shame engulfed her and she swept up an unsteady hand to detach his fingers from her hair and pull back. 'I know there are no guarantees in life but that's not enough for me,' she said tautly.

'This is beginning to sound like a negotiation and negotiations invariably end with a price.'

'Feelings don't come with prices attached.'

He threw back his arrogant dark head, ebony brows raised in challenge above cool, watchful black eyes. 'Are you sure of that? I've already given up my freedom and, strange as it might seem to you, that feels like a pretty hefty concession when I've never done it before.'

Refusing to be driven into retreat by the warning chill in the air, Rosie tilted her chin. 'You haven't given up anything for my benefit. You only married me because of the will and we're only here together now because the Press found out. Do you have any idea how that makes me feel? Well, I'll tell you how it makes me feel...like the flavour of the month for a casual sexual interlude,' she asserted with steadily rising volume in the face of his dauntingly impassive appraisal. 'And it might surprise you but I value myself a lot more highly than that!'

A silence punctuated by the audible hiss of her quickened breathing fell.

'Then we would appear to have nothing more to discuss,' Constantine concluded softly.

Rosie frowned in bemusement. 'But...'

Constantine elevated a winged brow. 'You don't want a casual sexual interlude...and I don't want anything else.'

The flush on Rosie's cheeks slowly drained away, leaving her as white as his shirt-front. That cold-blooded assurance cut right into her like a knife. Nothing had ever hurt her so much. She clambered out of the Ferrari like a drunk trying to act sober, choosing each movement with infinitesimal care. Her stomach churned with nausea.

She could not believe that she had clumsily exposed herself to that level of rejection. Like a frantic teenager in love, she had slung her fear and insecurity at him in the hope of drawing a reassuring response. But Constantine did not appreciate being put on the spot and he had had no inhibitions about brutally matching her foolish candour.

'Of course,' Constantine added softly, smoothly as he studied the rigidity of her slender back, 'you could always try to change my mind, *pethi mou*.'

Rosie shuddered as the knife slid deeper still into her unprotected heart. In that selfsame moment, she also learnt that when provoked she could still hate almost as much as she loved.

'And permit me to offer some advice,' he murmured. 'You are not going to do it by chasing off down a mountain with the throwback.'

Rosie lifted her fiery head high and turned round to face him again. 'As far as I'm concerned, you don't exist any more. You are beneath my notice,' she stated with tremulous, driven dignity. 'And I don't want anything more to do with you.'

Anguished pain and flagellated pride weighted her as she walked indoors, shoulders square, chin high. Maybe it was just as well that she had been so painfully and naïvely frank, she told herself heavily. At last she now knew where she stood. And she knew how he saw her now too. She might not have enjoyed having her worst suspicions confirmed but knowledge was protection . . . *wasn't it*?

'Oh, you shouldn't have!' Rosie scolded when she glanced up and found Carmina hovering over her with a glass of freshly squeezed lemonade. 'I could have come inside to get something.'

'When you are inside?' the old lady grumbled. 'You come inside only when it is getting dark.'

Standing up, Rosie straightened, and her aching back protested. She rubbed her damp hands down over her grubby shorts and grasped the glass with a determined smile. 'This garden . . . it's beginning to look good again, don't you think?'

Carmina settled down on the flight of stone steps rediscovered only the day before as a result of Rosie's industrious labour and folded her plump arms. Her wrinkled face was troubled as she surveyed the pruned shrubs and the border of old climbing roses which now stood revealed where there had once been only a tangled thicket of undergrowth. She sighed. 'The marriage . . . it is not looking so good.'

Wincing, Rosie tilted her tense face up to the sun and then drank deep of the lemonade. It quenched her thirst but the effort of forcing liquid past her tightening throat muscles hurt. 'Carmina—'

'This is not what your father wanted,' Carmina told her stubbornly. 'You and Constantine . . . this marriage was his dream for the future.'

'Dreams don't always work out . . .' In fact, Anton's dream had plunged her into a real nightmare, Rosie reflected wretchedly.

Over the past three days, living under the same roof as Constantine had become an agonising ordeal and no matter how hard she tried she had found it impossible to rise above that rejection and behave as if nothing had happened. She just couldn't bear to be in the same room as him. She just couldn't bear to look at him or speak to him. She could only suppress her turbulent emotions in hard physical work, and at night she was so darned tired, she ought to have been sleeping like the dead . . . but she *wasn't*.

She tossed, she turned and then she slid into an uneasy doze, only to wake up in hot-faced shock from dream after erotic dream about Constantine. What she did to him, what he did to her and the incredible number of unlikely places in which they carried out these shameless fantasies of hers ensured that her nights were far more exhausting than her days. And her inventive imagination made it even more impossible for her to meet Constantine's eyes.

'He does not know that you are Don Antonio's daughter,' Carmina complained in a tone of reproof. 'That is a very big secret to keep from your husband.'

'I know what I'm doing, Carmina.'

'How can you say that? There is no peace in Son Fontanal. We all creep about the house...no smiles, no laughter. That fancy cook...he says if one more meal comes back to him uneaten he will leave!'

'Constantine has a filthy temper.'

'With a wife labouring in the garden all day, he has reason. You are neglecting your husband.'

Not in her dreams, she wasn't. 'He thrives on neglect.'

With a disapproving clicking of her teeth, Carmina shook her head and got up to go. 'You are as stubborn as he is.'

Rosie settled back down to her weeding with renewed vigour. If her father was looking down on her and Constantine now, she knew he would be blaming her too. But from the moment that Constantine had asserted that had she been related to Anton he would have felt obligated to stay married to her Rosie had been determined not to try to attract and hold him on that basis.

Having smoothly seduced her into bed, Constantine had then freely admitted that his sole interest in her was sexual. Had he known she was Anton's daughter, he would have tried to pretend that there was more to their relationship but all the time he would've been feeling trapped and resenting her like mad. And to try to tell him now when they were at daggers drawn and when she had no real proof to offer...what would be the point?

'Why did you send away the gardeners I engaged?'

Startled, Rosie twisted round on her knees. A big black shadow had blocked out the sun. She focused on

Constantine's hand-stitched Italian loafers and looked no higher. 'I prefer to do the work myself.'

'There are several acres of ground here.'

'Well, I've got plenty of time on my hands, haven't I?' Her treacherous gaze started wandering up from the hem of his beautifully tailored grey trousers to the extensive length of his lean, hard thighs. Her stomach clenched and turned over.

Constantine released his breath in an explosive hiss. 'You won't go out to lunch, you won't go out to dinner... you won't even go out for a drive...'

They did nothing so safe in Rosie's night-time fantasies. Her guilt-stricken appraisal strayed to the hard, muscular flare of his hip and the taut flatness of his stomach then lower again and she closed her eyes in absolute anguish as she realised that she was eating him up with her eyes. 'I'd be wasting my time and yours.'

'You nourish a grievance like a child revelling in a monumental sulk!'

'I'm not sulking. I just don't think we have anything left to say to each other. You said it *all*.'

'*Christos*... at least stand up and look at me when you're speaking to me!' Constantine grated rawly, bending down without warning to close one strong hand over hers and tug her upright.

Rosie pulled herself free and backed away several steps. Involuntarily her evasive gaze clashed with diamond-hard dark eyes. It was even worse than she had feared. That collision cost her dear. It was like being run over by a truck, thrown into the air with heart fearfully hammering and the breath wrenched from her body, all control wrested from her.

She shivered, every muscle taut as the hunger hit her in a stormy, greedy wave, a desperate, obsessive wanting that paid no heed to pride or intelligence. She wanted to touch him so badly, her fingernails bit sharp crescents into her hands. The simmering tension in the atmosphere heightened, until she could hear the accelerated thump of her heart in her ears.

'What I said to you...' Brilliant dark golden eyes challenged her levelly, his sensual mouth twisting. 'Has it occurred to you that perhaps I wasn't ready to answer questions about us?'

She wanted to believe him—she wanted to believe him so badly, she could almost taste her own desperation. But it had taken him too long to come up with that justification and suddenly Rosie despised herself for even listening. She started walking away. 'I need a bath—'

A lean hand whipped out and closed round her forearm to stay her. 'Is that all you have to say to me?' he gritted.

Angry green eyes flashed into his. 'You miscalculated, Constantine. You're so used to saying and doing whatever you like with women that you thought you could do the same with me.'

'What the hell are you talking about?' he growled.

A bitter little laugh was dredged from her tight throat. 'You assumed that you could be honest and get away with it. In fact, not only did you think that, you actually thought that putting me down would make me try harder to please...' Her strained voice shook and she compressed her lips to silence herself.

For a split second, Constantine stared down at her, inky black lashes low on his stabbing gaze. 'That is not true—'

'I don't believe you. You're arrogant and selfish and inconsiderate of other people's feelings,' Rosie asserted unsteadily. 'And I don't care how rich or how powerful you are...I wouldn't give daylight to any man who talked to me like that!'

'Is that a fact?' Reaching out for her with two determined hands, Constantine urged her up against him and sent every skin cell in her taut body leaping. 'You will give me a lot more than daylight before I am finished, *pethi mou!*'

His vengeful mouth was hot, hungry and hard and her knees gave way. His tongue delved between her lips with an erotic thrust that tore a whimper of delight from her. Raw excitement electrified her, releasing the uncontrollable flood of her own hunger. She shuddered convulsively and her heart raced so hard and fast that she clung and clutched at him to stay upright.

And then just as suddenly she was freed, left to find her own support on wildly wobbling legs, dilated green eyes pinned to him in shock. That separation was as painful and as unwelcome as an amputation when every shameless, sensitised inch of her quivering body craved more—so much more that she was in torment.

She focused in appalled fascination on the grimy set of fingerprints which now marred his silk shirt, sweeping up from his waist, glancing across his broad chest in an obviously lingering caress and then indenting clearly across his wide shoulders where she had clung. Those marks were now exhibited for all to see, like a public badge of her shame and surrender.

'You need to change your shirt,' she mumbled shakily.

'I shall wear it with pride,' Constantine confided with disconcerting amusement. 'There don't seem to be many parts of me that you overlooked—'

'Change it,' Rosie muttered in a heartfelt plea, hurriedly sidestepping him to head back towards the house. 'I'm going for a bath.'

'I'll see you upstairs,' Constantine murmured smoothly.

She stiffened and then grasped his meaning. He had to change and half his clothes were in the wardrobe in her room, even though he slept in a bedroom across the landing. Her head was still spinning. One kiss and she had been so far gone, Constantine could have done anything with her! Not a bit of wonder he was laughing! She was his for the taking and he knew it.

A taxi was waiting in the courtyard and as Rosie entered the hall a maid was showing a grey-haired man with a briefcase into the drawing room. Momentarily, the man stilled, shooting Rosie an almost startled glance. Then, just as abruptly, his keen dark eyes veiled and he inclined his head in a polite nod of acknowledgement before disappearing from her view.

Rosie looked curiously at Dmitri where he stood below the stairs. 'Who was that?'

'Theodopoulos Stephanos. Mr Voulos's lawyer.'

No doubt the man had stared because she looked such a fright in her gardening clothes . . . hardly the image he might have expected from Constantine's wife, temporary or otherwise.

In the bathroom, she stripped off. An agony of self-loathing engulfed her and for long, anguished minutes she simply stood there, tasting the painful reality of her supreme unimportance in Constantine's life . . .

Not a wife, not a girlfriend, not even a mistress. You're a puddle of self-pity, a little inner voice scolded drily as she washed herself. Maybe he *had been* telling the truth when he'd said he just hadn't been ready to answer questions about their relationship. Maybe, in her defensive insecurity, she was her own worst enemy. Angry confusion shrilled through her then. Now she was making excuses for Constantine and blaming herself!

Anchoring a fleecy towel round her in a careless swathe, she walked back into the bedroom . . . and stopped dead. Her bed was occupied. Constantine was in it, every muscular line of his lithe body fluidly indolent, his bronzed skin startlingly dark against the pale bedlinen. Eyes huge, Rosie gaped at him. A smile of intense amusement curled his wickedly sensual mouth.

'I don't know what you think you're doing here—'

'*Theos*...' Constantine ran deceptively sleepy eyes of gold over her and her heart took a frantic, convulsive leap against her breastbone. 'You need me to state my intentions?'

'I've got a very fair idea of your intentions, Constantine,' Rosie spluttered, stalking over to the door, intending to throw it wide in an invitation for him to leave.

'It's locked.'

Rosie spun round. Constantine displayed a large, ornate key for her inspection. 'We wouldn't want to startle the staff again.'

'Give me that key!' Rosie launched at him furiously.

'Come and get it...'

Rosie hesitated.

Constantine dealt her a wolfish grin, white teeth gleaming against golden skin. 'Didn't I tell you that you'd learn caution around me?'

That one taunt was sufficient to overcome it. Rosie landed on the bed in a flying leap of temper and made a wild snatch at the key. Constantine flung it across the room and snaked two powerful arms round her slender waist to entrap her. 'I knew you would rise to the bait.'

Clamped to his hard, lean length in impotent stillness, Rosie flung her fiery head back and glowered down at him. 'Let go of me!'

'Self-denial doesn't come naturally to me. And I wouldn't say that you were a rousing success in that department either.' Constantine surveyed her with thickly lashed eyes screened to a mocking sliver of knowing gold. 'Ten hours a day with a hoe you use like a machete! I have to confess that no woman has ever gone to that amount of effort to resist me, *pethi mou*.'

'I just don't want to be anywhere near you!' Rosie snarled, feeling the naked heat of his intimidatingly relaxed length striking her through the thin sheet and the rumpled towel that separated them. Terrifying little shivers of seething sexual awareness were already pulling her skin tight over her bones and strangling her breathing processes.

'Because you don't trust yourself,' Constantine savoured with raw satisfaction. 'And, watching you bend and stretch in those shorts, I was equally challenged. You have the most provocative heart-shaped derrière, little rag-doll...and when you shake your T-shirt because you're getting too warm those beautiful little breasts bounce and push against the damp cotton until your nipples—'

'Stop it!' Appalled to realise that he had been watching her and noticing such things, Rosie was mortified.

Brilliant dark golden eyes intent, Constantine appraised the hot pink flush on her cheeks. 'You still blush like an innocent. That turns me on even harder,' he confided huskily as he fluidly shifted to kick the sheet away and yanked at her towel to detach it.

Taken by surprise, Rosie made a mad grab at her only covering just a second too late and found herself swung over lightning-fast onto her back with Constantine looking down at her instead. *'No!'*

'Christos...you smell of soap—all clean and scrubbed and sweet. But even when you're dirty and sweaty and too warm you excite me. The scent of you, the feel of you, the *taste* of you,' he growled sexily, a lean, hair-roughened thigh deftly parting hers as he brought his weight down on her and shamelessly acquainted her with the smooth, hard thrust of his erection.

A burst of burning heat ignited low in the pit of Rosie's stomach. 'Your lawyer's waiting to see you downstairs!' she gasped in sudden recall, fighting her own weakness with all her might.

'Theo's already gone.' A slight frown drew Constantine's winged brows together. 'Crazy of him to come all this way only to deliver some papers and then refuse to even stay for lunch.' Golden eyes smouldered down at her hectically flushed face. 'But remarkably tactful.'

Transfixed, Rosie stared back up at him, great rolling breakers of excitement making her heart thunder and her limbs quiver. Her breasts felt swollen and tender, the taut peaks aching for his mouth and his hands, and never had she been more agonisingly aware of the moist, throbbing centre of need between her thighs.

'We don't need other people around us, *pethi mou*. They get in the way and I am far too distracted to work. Say something,' Constantine invited encouragingly.

Rosie parted dry lips and managed only one word, so intense was her arousal. '*Please...*'

Primitive triumph flashed in his glittering gaze. He ran slow, seeking fingers over the pouting mounds he had bared for his pleasure. As his thumbs glanced over the stiff pink buds straining up to him, she gasped and rose against him, every nerve-ending in her body screaming in response. He thrust her flat with a devouringly passionate kiss. She kissed him back with desperate urgency, everything she had held back for long, endless days suddenly betraying her in a stormy flood of possessive need. Her hands ran over him, smoothing over warm golden skin sheathing whipcord muscles, and a hungry moan of impatience escaped her.

'You are always in a rush...'

Rosie twisted and squirmed, on fire with wanting him, not a shred of self-restraint left or even recalled. Clenching her fingers into his thick, silky black hair, she shifted her legs in an aching invitation more blatant than speech.

With an urgent groan, Constantine sank his hands to her hips and hauled her under him. Then he hesitated. 'I don't want to hurt you again.'

'You don't argue with me in my fantasies...you don't stop...you don't make me wait!' Rosie sobbed in explosive frustration.

The silence thundered. She closed her eyes in horror. Oh, no, I didn't say that...*did I*? she asked herself.

'What do I do?' he murmured.

'What I want,' Rosie mumbled.

Constantine vented a ragged laugh of appreciation. The velvet-hard thrust of him surged teasingly against her, gently probing the slick, damp welcome awaiting him.

Rosie was on a high of such shivering excitement, she couldn't have vocalised to save her life. What she wanted was even more thrilling in reality. He entered her so slowly that she raked her fingernails down his back. The pleasure was so intoxicatingly intense, she lost herself in the bold feel of him stretching her with delicious force.

'Open your eyes,' Constantine ordered.

Rosie lifted lush lashes to see the blazing gold command in his eyes and drowned. She was drugged into silence by sensation, feverish, all-absorbing sensation, as he withdrew and then thrust into her all over again. He was slow and then fast, smooth and then rough. She couldn't do anything but cling with impassioned hands and moan and sob her incredible pleasure. He went on and on and on, driving her to mindless heights until the pulsing, tormenting heat inside her exploded and unleashed a shattering tidal wave of satisfaction.

As he shuddered in the protective circle of her arms, an aching flood of tenderness consumed Rosie and she pressed her lips lovingly to a smooth brown shoulder.

Drinking in the hot, musky scent of his damp skin, she felt utterly at peace.

Constantine released her from his weight and bent over her. 'Where are you under all that hair?' he groaned, lean fingers brushing the tangle of bright curls gently off her brow.

Compelling dark eyes probed her dreamy face. His fingertips lightly traced the delicate curve of her jawbone and she turned her cheek slowly into his palm, a wondering light in her gaze as she recalled his eagerness to leave her the first time they had made love. In the heart-stopping silence, he rearranged a straying curl to his own satisfaction and let his thumb lightly caress the reddened pout of her lower lip.

He collided with her fascinated scrutiny and a faint, rueful smile curved his wide mouth. 'I can't stop touching you...'

That charismatic smile turned her heart over and inside out.

'And I want you all over again,' he confided.

As he pulled her back into his arms, she quivered in helpless response. Her fingers delved into his luxuriant hair. Held fast by his dark golden eyes, she was conscious of an extraordinary surge of happiness.

'It was a really good idea to give the staff the rest of the day off,' Rosie mused, seated on the edge of the scrubbed table, watching Constantine struggle to find a tidy way of finishing off the doorstep-sized sandwich she had made. 'But I didn't realise you would be so helpless without a chef.'

Constantine looked wary. 'I thought you could cook.'

'I know, and look where it got you. I live on salad, fruit and convenience food. Your chef does not use convenience food and he deserves a medal for serving up such wonderful menus on that prehistoric cooker. Still, at least I can make coffee,' she murmured with dancing eyes, flicking a meaningful glance at the undrinkable tarry brew he had prepared when challenged.

'You also look very good on a kitchen table,' Constantine told her.

Rosie swung up her jean-clad legs and lay on her side, posing like a fifties film starlet, her bright head propped on the heel of her hand. A slow smile curved his mouth and he laughed. 'You like sending me up, don't you?'

'You've only just realised?'

'Slow learner,' he murmured, studying her with appreciative eyes as she slid in one fluid, impulsive movement off the table again. 'But I hope you're not heading for a window, *pethi mou.*'

'A window?' And then she reddened and ran her fingers restively through her hair, recalling the manner in which she had left his home in Greece and the quick escape she had made the day she'd gone down the mountain with Maurice.

'In certain moods you're like a cat burglar.'

'I've had a lot of practice over the years.' She laughed uneasily, not liking the turn the conversation had taken.

'Running away? It's a waste of time with me,' Constantine informed her with deep conviction. 'The more you run, the harder I chase. It's an elemental response. I can't seem to beat it.'

'You just want to catch up with me so that you can tell me what you think of me for doing it in the first place.'

'You only do it when I have upset you,' he returned with a perception that shook her. 'Or got too close. Now I can stop doing the first but I'm definitely not going to stop doing the second.'

'Is that a threat?'

He tugged her into his arms with insistent hands. 'I don't make threats any more,' he said softly. 'I make promises. I want to know everything there is to know about you, *agape mou.*'

The tenderness in his steady dark appraisal made her heart sing. He was being so open, so honest. A little twinge of shame filled her as she lowered her own gaze. She was the one with the secrets, not him. Soon she would need to tell him all over again that she was Anton's daughter... but not just at this moment when she was revelling in the awareness that he couldn't take his eyes off her.

The thunderous slam of a door jolted Rosie awake. Blinking bemusedly in the lamplight, she pulled herself up against the pillows and focused hazily on Constantine where he stood at the foot of the bed, bare-chested, only a pair of faded tight jeans riding low on his lean hips. A tender smile curved her lips. He looked so spectacular, he *always* looked so spectacular, that she could even forgive him for carelessly wakening her up from the first sound sleep she had enjoyed in days.

Ferocious dark eyes slashed into hers. Rosie stiffened in dismay, her smile dying, her tummy muscles clenching. Seething tension emanated from Constantine in waves.

'What's wrong?' she whispered.

'I was hungry. I got up to get something to eat and on the way downstairs I began wondering what was so important about those papers that Theo thought it necessary to fly over and personally place them in my hands... and if they *were* worthy of that importance why didn't he say so and why was he so keen to make an exit again?'

Rosie's attention slowly dropped to the bulky brown envelope clasped in one lean brown hand. Her heart jumped into her mouth.

'But now I understand. Theo was embarrassed,' Constantine continued in the same murderously quiet drawl.

'Because when I gave him the licence to empty a certain safety-deposit box held in Anton's name neither one of us was expecting anything of a confidential nature to emerge...'

He lifted his other hand and something fluttered down onto the bed. Rosie snatched the item up. Her hand trembled. She was looking at a small colour snap of herself as a toddler.

Black eyes blazed condemnation at her, his lean, dark features clenched hard. 'You wanted revenge, didn't you? You were going to wait right to the bitter end to throw your paternity in my face!'

CHAPTER TEN

REVENGE? Stunned by the accusation, Rosie reacted on instinct. Sliding out of bed at speed, she made an unwittingly pleading movement towards Constantine.

'Forget it. The last thing on my mind right now is that deceptively tempting little body of yours!' Constantine asserted with biting derision.

Swept by abrasive dark eyes, Rosie suddenly felt appallingly naked. She grabbed up the towel lying on the rug by the bed and hurriedly wrapped it around her. 'Where did you get that photo from?'

In answer, Constantine withdrew a whole handful of photos from the envelope and cast them down on the mattress like a thrown gauntlet. 'Rosie from birth to the age of nine. And not a happy child according to this pictorial account. You've got tears in your eyes in half of them and what look like slap marks all down your leg on another.' His deep, dark drawl wavered slightly and his eloquent mouth compressed hard. 'I imagine Anton was suitably tortured in receipt of such heartbreaking reminders of your existence. *Theos* . . . your mother must've been bitter!'

'Maybe.' Her tortured breath caught in her throat. 'I did try to tell you who I was—'

'And your mother taught you that same bitterness,' Constantine stabbed as if she hadn't spoken, murderously bright golden eyes lancing into her.

'What are you talking about?'

'You were planning to unveil yourself as Anton's child only when Thespina was present to enjoy the full effect of your revelation.'

Rosie's eyes flew wide, shock freezing her facial muscles. 'I would never have done that! *Never!*'

'Well, you certainly weren't about to waste any time trying to convince me of your true identity, not once you'd had the opportunity to think the idea over,' Constantine condemned between gritted teeth. 'Keeping quiet was much more fun, wasn't it?'

Hopelessly confused by his attacks, Rosie gasped, 'I still don't understand—'

In one powerful stride, Constantine reached her and closed two strong hands round her slender forearms to force her closer. '*Christos*... you were waiting for your moment and hoping to cause the maximum damage. You weren't prepared that day in London when Thespina arrived without warning. But you told me—you just blurted it out like a bad joke and then you never referred to the subject again. OK, I didn't listen, but you made no real attempt to convince me that you were serious! What was I supposed to think?'

'I had no way of making you believe me. I have no proof of who I am!' Rosie protested fiercely.

'Anton had the proof and you must have known that. You didn't even care that this file might have fallen into Thespina's hands!' In unconcealed disgust, Constantine thrust her back from him again.

'I didn't even think about it, for heaven's sake. Do you think I was *expecting* my father to die?' Rosie prompted jerkily. 'And Anton never mentioned any file to me... What's in it?'

'Your history from birth. Evidently he knew every damn thing about you before he even approached you!'

The news shattered Rosie. There had been so many painful events in her life which she had deliberately not shared with her father. She had wanted to protect him. And yet all the time he had known exactly what her life had been like.

'How did Anton get involved with your mother?' Constantine demanded.

Rosie's legs wouldn't hold her up any longer. She sank down dizzily on the side of the bed. 'His secretary was sick. Mum was an agency temp. Their affair only lasted a few weeks before he finished it—'

'Because my parents died and Anton and Thespina became my legal guardians. I imagine you've often thought how *very* different your life might have been had that not happened.'

It was strange, Rosie registered in deep shock, but she had never made that final connection until Constantine made it for her. Almost twenty-one years ago, she had been accidentally conceived when Anton's marriage was on the rocks. And then ironically, within weeks of her conception, a tragic car crash had quite miraculously given her father and his wife the child they had both been longing for. A nine-year-old boy had become their shared responsibility and had effectively healed the breach between them. And that little boy had been Constantine.

'I never appreciated that timing before...not properly,' she admitted tautly. 'But Anton had no idea that my mother was pregnant when they parted. He didn't find out until it was far too late for him to try and help her.'

'No, he got a photo and a cold little note through the post telling him that he was the father of a daughter he could never know because your mother had married another man. When the photos stopped coming, I assume that he couldn't live with his curiosity any longer and he started looking for you.'

'He didn't even know my stepfather's name... he had so little to go on and a couple of times he gave up.'

'*Christos* . . . you must hate *me* as much as you hate Thespina for the life you have led!' Constantine ground out half under his breath. He swung violently away from her as if he could no longer bear to look at her. Every powerful line of his lean, muscular body sizzled with whip-taut tension.

'I don't hate anyone.' But Rosie still felt ashamed because she could remember occasions before her father's death when her resentment of his legitimate family had risen to explosive proportions . . . only that had been before she had met Constantine and Thespina and before she had made herself face reality.

'Anton didn't love my mother,' she pointed out tightly. 'He never stopped loving Thespina. Even if he had known about me, he wouldn't have divorced her for my mother. I think she knew that and that's why she never gave him a choice.'

'You didn't give *me* a choice either,' Constantine condemned with ringing bitterness. 'You allowed me to go on thinking that you had slept with Anton. Even when you knew that that belief was tearing me apart, you let me go on believing it!'

'I kept on telling you that we weren't lovers—'

'While being aware that that made no kind of sense! The only other possible explanation for Anton's will was the one I came up with. And you only have yourself to thank for the way I treated you.' His hawk-like profile rigid with repressed emotion, Constantine dealt her a raw-edged glance. 'But I have to live with the awareness that I cruelly and cynically misjudged Anton and did everything I could to evade the responsibility that he trusted me to accept. And that responsibility was for his daughter. I betrayed his trust in every way possible.'

'You didn't betray anything . . . it was outrageous of him to demand that you marry me!' Her anxious eyes clung to the fierce cast of his features. 'I know he had good intentions but it was still crazy!'

'I was one bloody mixed-up kid when the Estradas got landed with me... They put up with me and straightened me out. Without their love and guidance, I'd have gone off the rails. You can never repay a debt like that.' Pale beneath his dark skin, Constantine compressed his lips and turned away from her again to stride over to the window and yank open the curtains on the clear moonlit night beyond. The savage tension in his wide brown shoulders made her drop her aching eyes.

It was something of a shock for Rosie to appreciate that Constantine's early years with his own parents might have been less than perfect. Yet she remembered him admitting that Anton had meant more to him than his own father. She stifled her curiosity because she was already squirming with all kinds of incredibly guilty feelings. Constantine had interpreted her silence as evidence of malice and a vengeful desire to put him in the wrong. He had even cherished the suspicion that she had been lying in wait for some kind of spiteful showdown with Thespina.

'I'm sorry...maybe I should've spoken up again sooner, but you really cut me off that day when I tried to tell you, and then later, when you started talking about debts and stuff,' Rosie framed tremulously, 'I just couldn't face—'

Abruptly, Constantine wheeled round and strode back across the room. Alarmingly strong hands closed over her shoulders and dragged her upright. Blazing golden eyes swept her shaken face in smouldering fury. 'You were a virgin...but you would have died sooner than give me the pleasure of knowing that you had not been Anton's woman first! Every way you could, you turned the screw on me! What a cold, vindictive bitch you are,' he grated thickly. 'And what a bloody fool I was to think differently!'

As the door thudded shut on his exit, Rosie stood there with slow, painful tears tracking down her quivering cheeks. Only hours earlier she had gone to sleep in his arms. She had felt so close to him, so...cherished. *Cherished?* A hiccuping sob escaped her, and then another. Why did she kid herself like that? Why was she so wretchedly naïve? So Constantine was fantastic in bed and he was experienced enough to make a woman feel incredibly special, but that was *all*. It didn't mean he had been falling in love with her or wanting to make their marriage a real one.

And now, he despised her. It had never occurred to her that the information she was withholding might have such a devastating emotional effect on him. What had she expected? Well, at the very least she had expected the chance to tell him herself and she had expected him to be incredulous and then probably apologising all over the place for not believing her claim the first time she had made it.

Constantine...filled with remorse and humility, shamefacedly apologising? Rosie squirmed. At the back of her mind, hadn't she been looking forward to that highly imaginative moment and feeling slightly smug that he was in for a major shock? Hadn't she been determined that he should want her for herself and not because she was Anton's daughter? And hadn't she even secretly hoped that by the time she got around to breaking the news at a carefully chosen optimum moment it might finally strike Constantine as *terrific* news? She winced in remembrance.

All along she had blithely ignored the nature of the male animal she was dealing with. In her hurt pride and insecurity, she had been selfish and insensitive. Constantine made a real virtue of candour and plain speaking. Her continued silence *had* been a form of deception and he could scarcely be blamed for assuming the worst about her motives.

After pacing the floor for what felt like hours, Rosie tried to get some sleep, but she found it impossible to still her uneasy conscience or to suppress the suspicion that she had made a poor showing in her own defence. Switching on the bedside light, she discovered that it was almost three in the morning. Would Constantine be asleep? Or would he be lying awake like she was?

Clad in a faded cotton nightshirt, Rosie tiptoed across the landing and slowly opened the door. Moonlight shone through the windows onto the untouched bed. From the stairs, she saw a dim light showing beneath the drawing-room door. In the hall she hesitated, wondering what on earth she was going to say when she couldn't bring herself to admit that she was head over heels in love with him...

Right now he hated her, and even if he got over that aversion the announcement that she was in love with him might scare him all the way back to Greece. A male who had never been in love and who was extremely wary of commitment was unlikely to feel comfortable with being loved, even by a temporary wife, who would be lying in her teeth if she said she didn't have a hidden agenda.

Rosie tilted her chin and opened the door. Only one lamp was lit, leaving most of the vast room in gloomy dark shadow. Constantine was lying on a sofa. She crept over to him just as he muttered something slurred in Greek. His dense black lashes lifted and it appeared to be a struggle for him to focus on her.

'Constantine?'

He blinked twice, a slow frown drawing his ebony brows together, and he responded to his name in his own language.

His black hair was tousled and a heavy blue-black shadow of stubble obscured his hard jawline. But it was the look of desolation in his eyes which punched a hole in Rosie's heart. She dropped down on her knees by the sofa and reached for one lean brown hand. 'I'm so sor—'

A flicker of movement stirred in the shadows and Rosie gasped, almost jumping out of her skin. Having risen from his seat behind the door, Dmitri strolled forward. 'I'll look after him, Mrs Voulos.'

'Is he ill? I mean...' She fell silent as she belatedly picked up the strong smell of alcohol. Her attention skimmed to the whisky bottle and glass lying abandoned on the rug and she froze in dismayed comprehension. 'He's...*he's*—?'

'A little under the weather. Go back to bed,' Dmitri urged flatly. 'I'll stay with him.'

'Does he make a habit of this?' Rosie managed shakily, her small fingers curving possessively round one lean, unresponsive thigh.

'I have never seen him like this before.' Even in shock that Constantine could do something as uncharacteristic as get paralytically drunk, Rosie would have had to be blind to miss the coolness in the older man's eyes and the protective way he hovered at the head of the sofa, as if she were some sort of a threat to his employer's safety.

'What's he talking about?' she pressed as Constantine shifted and muttered some more.

'Rabbits,' Dmitri informed her with extreme reluctance.

'Rabbits?' Rosie queried weakly.

'I'll take him up to bed...' Dmitri stepped forward, forcing Rosie to relinquish her hold and scramble upright.

'I'll help you.'

'Thank you but that won't be necessary.'

Rosie backed away, dismayed by the bodyguard's barely concealed hostility. He hesitated, clearly determined not to subject Constantine to the indignity of his assistance while she lingered. From the door, she glanced back. 'It's not the way you think it is,' she said helplessly.

'It's not my place to think anything, Mrs Voulos.'

But condemnation was written all over him, his usual quiet friendliness chilled out by what she recognised as fierce defensive loyalty to Constantine. Only the conviction that Constantine was too damned macho and proud to want her around him when he was in that condition spurred Rosie back to her room.

She lay in bed, watching dawn break the skies. He was really upset . . . he had to be to have drunk like that. And Rosie tried so hard to understand. Wasn't she herself equally guilty of betraying Anton's trust? She had only agreed to marry Constantine under duress, and would have run a thousand miles had she known what fate had in store for them in the morning after the ceremony.

And it wasn't as if Constantine had tried to disinherit her or anything like that. Anton had got himself into serious financial hot water raising the loan for the Son Fontanal estate. Constantine must have used his own money to bail out his guardian's business ventures and even the house needed a fortune spent on it. Indeed being Anton's heir had undoubtedly proved to be a most unprofitable undertaking, but Constantine, famed in the business world for his ruthless pursuit of profit, would never admit that because to do so would be disloyal.

So why had her Greek tycoon drunk himself into a stupor? Guilt at not rolling out a red carpet for Anton's daughter? Or suicidal depression at the knowledge that if he carried out his guardian's last wishes he would be stuck with Rosie for ever?

Her sensitive stomach lurching, she got out of bed again. Pulling on jeans and a fresh cotton top, she paused only to drag a brush through her mane of fiery hair. She needed some fresh air and space. The motorbike she had hired was parked below the steps in the courtyard. She hadn't been out on it since her arrival and maybe a ride down that mountain would blow the cobwebs away...

It was still very early when Rosie stopped in the shade of some sweet-smelling pine trees and ate the snack she had brought with her. The canned drink and the long bread roll filled with ham and luscious wedges of tomato satisfied her appetite but the hollow feeling inside her wouldn't go away. She was struggling desperately hard to convince herself that there would be life after Constantine. What did they have in common, after all?

He was a domineering, arrogant, workaholic tycoon. He was everything she wasn't. Rich, educated, pedigreed. He was far better-looking than she was. He also had loads of women running after him and Rosie was not the type to compete in a race. She had her pride, not to mention the painful experience of being brought down to earth with a severe bump only hours earlier.

If Constantine had had any feelings for her, she had killed them. So there was no point in concentrating on the more positive aspects of his personality. Like the fact that he could be incredibly charming and entertaining and give the most astonishing impression of being caring and supportive. That sort of stuff wasn't relevant. That was her foolish heart talking, not her head. They didn't have a real marriage. And their temporary arrangement was currently at breaking point.

A big black shiny limousine was parked outside Son Fontanal. Rosie rode past it into the courtyard and slowly, stiffly dismounted. She was removing her helmet when Constantine strode down the steps. Her treacherous heart performed a somersault. Attired as he was in an Italian-cut double-breasted cream suit that highlighted his black hair and golden skin, one look made her melt like chocolate left out in the sun.

Brilliant dark eyes swept over her and lingered, a curious stillness etched into his strong, dark face. 'Did it even occur to you that I might be worried sick about you?'

Rosie reddened with discomfiture. 'I was away before I thought about that.'

'Where the hell did you get the bike?'

'I hired it for a fortnight the day I arrived.'

'I assumed it belonged to one of the workmen. Dmitri will see that it is returned. I don't like the idea of you out on a motorbike on these roads,' Constantine delivered, the faint pallor beneath his sun-bronzed complexion emphasising the tense line of his mouth.

As he stared at her, holding her there by sheer force of will, the silence mounted, thick and heavy. And suddenly she understood. He hadn't thought she would be coming back but for some reason he wasn't saying one half of what he wanted to say on that subject.

'Thespina arrived ten minutes ago,' he breathed in taut explanation.

Rosie stiffened and lost every scrap of colour. 'Oh, no...'

'I have decided that we have no option other than to tell her the truth,' he admitted with grim emphasis. 'Too many people know your identity now. A slip of the tongue and any lies or half-truths would be exposed. I cannot take that risk.'

Shock glued Rosie's feet to the worn paving stones. Constantine closed a big hand round hers and drew her up the steps into the hall. Rosie tried to pull free then. '*You* do it!'

'This particular confession needs to come from both of us, *pethi mou*.' His lean fingers retaining their determined grip, Constantine led her into the drawing room before she could utter another word of argument.

Thespina rose to greet her with a pleasant smile. Rosie's stomach lurched and sank to her toes. Oh, dear heaven, she just could not face what was to come!

'Come and sit down beside me,' Thespina invited, settling back onto the sofa and patting it cosily.

A maid entered with a tray and began to pour coffee. Positioning himself by the big stone fireplace, Constantine embarked on a somewhat strained conversation. Everyone having been served, the door closed on the maid.

Thespina turned to look at Rosie and, with a slow shake of her dark head, she said gently, 'I really feel this charade has gone on long enough. I have to confess that there was something rather endearing about Constantine's efforts to explain the inexplicable and protect me but I should've spoke up sooner. Even as a boy, he could never lie and look me in the eye.'

In the act of sugaring his coffee, Constantine straightened so fast that half the contents of his cup slopped onto the saucer. He set it down with a stifled oath. 'Are you saying that—?'

'I've known about Rosie's existence for almost twenty years,' Thespina confirmed, tactfully removing her gaze from Constantine's stunned visage and affecting not to hear Rosie's strangled gasp. 'You'll have to forgive me for not immediately recognising you, Rosalie. But I knew that you were Anton's child the instant Constantine said your name. The combination of your hair and that unusual name was too much for me to overlook and the two of you behaved very oddly. I'm afraid that I couldn't help but know that you weren't telling me the truth.'

'Twenty years...?' Constantine repeated in flat astonishment, still staring at the calm little Greek woman.

'Anton was never very good at hiding his feelings. He was dreadfully upset after he received that first photograph of Rosie,' Thespina proffered with a grimace. 'I found it in his desk with her mother's letter and then I understood. I was very distressed by what I learnt but in the end I was most concerned with keeping our marriage intact. I could've confronted him but what would I have achieved? His guilt and his fear of discovery were very obvious to me. I didn't want to lose him. Perhaps I was wrong not to bring it all out into the open—'

'No...he could not have handled that and stayed,' Constantine conceded half under his breath.

'He had already had so much to bear.' The older woman looked at Rosie and sighed heavily. 'All my life I'd received everything I wanted without effort. When my son was stillborn, when I finally had to accept that I was unlikely ever to give birth to a living child, I took my bitterness and my anger out on my husband and I rejected him. I told him I needed to be alone and I drove him away. I had less right than most to complain when he turned to another woman...'

Constantine frowned darkly. 'I had no idea your marriage had ever been in trouble.'

'It was before you came to us. And I allowed Rosie to remain a secret to conserve my own pride too. I also knew that her mother was married and I felt safe. As the years passed, I always made a point of seeking out those photos. Anton only placed them in a safety-deposit box shortly before he died.'

'All this time...you knew about me,' Rosie whispered in a daze.

'But it never occurred to me that Anton had found you. I was aware that he had attempted to trace you when you were younger and reached a dead end. When he became so buoyantly cheerful six months ago, I even suspected that he was having another affair.' Thespina surveyed the younger woman with wry but warm eyes. 'But I'm not sorry that he found you, Rosie. I'm glad that he was able to spend time with you before he died. I do know what that must have meant to him.'

Rosie licked her dry lips. 'You're being very understanding.'

'Secrets make everyone so uncomfortable,' Thespina pointed out ruefully. 'I am also now aware of the terms of my husband's new will. I would be *very* grateful if one of you would now tell me whether you are genuinely married or only pretending to be married for the sake of that will.'

Rosie swallowed the giant lump impeding her voice. 'We're faking it—'

'Like hell we are!' Constantine shot at Rosie in raw, angry disagreement.

'Perhaps I was a little premature with that question.' Setting down her empty coffee-cup with a faintly amused smile, Thespina stood up. 'But if you feel you could stay together long enough to supply me with a grandchild I would be very much obliged. I've been waiting a long time for that pleasure.'

Rosie studied her feet, burning colour in her cheeks. She couldn't bring herself to look at Constantine but she also realised what her father's widow was trying to tell her. Thespina was letting her know that she was ready to accept her as part of the family.

'Where are you going?' Constantine demanded of his stepmother.

'This was only intended as a flying visit to clear the air. I shall come back and see Son Fontanal some other time. By the way, Rosie...'

Rosie glanced up nervously. Thespina smiled again. 'Your father managed to persuade his mother not to sell the family portraits with the house. I would be happy to see them hung here where they belong.'

'Thespina could run rings around Machiavelli,' Rosie mumbled as the limousine disappeared from view. 'She wiped the floor with us both.'

Still in shock, she started back indoors. And then it hit her: Thespina knew everything. There was no further need for pretence, no necessity to wait before seeking a divorce. All of a sudden, Rosie's lower limbs felt like toothpicks struggling weakly to wade through a swamp. Thespina had dissolved the artificial boundaries within which their relationship had been formed. They had run out of time.

'How could you tell her that our marriage was a fake?' Constantine condemned wrathfully. 'Did you really think that was necessary?'

With difficulty, Rosie straightened her slumped shoulders and dug deep into her reserves of pride as she forced herself round to face him. 'I told the truth. After she had been so frank, anything less would have been an insult.'

Glittering black eyes centred on her with near-physical force. 'How was it the truth? Are we not married? Are we not lovers?'

Rosie's nerves were jangling like piano wires. 'You made it very clear how you felt about me last night.'

'*Christos* . . . I thought I did but now I'm not so sure. You put me through hell for no good reason. I may have wounded your pride by dismissing your claim to be Anton's daughter but you must have realised that the concept struck me as so incredible, I didn't even pause to consider it!' Shimmering dark eyes intercepted her evasive gaze. 'OK. . . I was in the wrong, but what I don't understand is your failure to repeat that claim once we knew each other better.'

'I didn't see that it would make any difference—'

'It would've made one hell of a difference if I'd known! And stop acting dumb!' Constantine bit out in frustration. 'I was shattered by the contents of that file. You seemed so open yet you had hidden the very essence of yourself from me...'

Her fingers clenched in on themselves as she faced the prospect of never seeing him again. Just walking away as if they had never been together, as if the past weeks had never happened. Acid burned her aching throat. The fear that she could not control her turbulent emotions drove her to say, 'It doesn't matter now, does it? We don't need to pretend for anyone's benefit now. We can get a divorce.'

Constantine perceptibly froze, his strong face clenching. 'I don't want a divorce.'

A great flood of pain and bitterness welled up inside Rosie, threatening her fast splintering control. And then the dam broke as she shot him a look of fierce condemnation. 'I'm not staying married to you just because you've got this stupid macho *thing* about keeping faith with what my father wanted!'

Constantine glowered at her in apparent incredulity. 'This is not a macho thing, Rosie,' he said drily.

A sob rollicked about like a death rattle in her chest. 'Call it what you like. I'm going upstairs to get packed!'

She raced out of the room and upstairs as if all the hounds of hell were on her trail. In fact they were inside her head. A weak, seductive little voice which she loathed was already pointing out that Constantine was offering himself on a plate. If he was stupid enough to do that and she wanted him, why shouldn't she hang onto him any way she could? Pride would be a cold, lonely bed-fellow and there was nothing cold about Constantine. She dashed an angry hand over her tear-filled eyes.

'Rosie...?'

'I'm not staying with you because you're great in bed either!' she blistered accusingly before she could bite the words back.

Thrusting the door shut and leaning back against it, his lean, powerful body rigid with tension, Constantine stared darkly back at her. 'But that attraction could be a beginning, a foundation—'

'Last night you called me a cold, vindictive bitch!' Rosie reminded him painfully.

Inky black lashes dropped low on fiercely intent golden eyes. '*Christos*, I didn't mean a word of it. I ... I was ...' He hesitated, teeth gritting. 'I was so...'

'You were what?' Rosie demanded.

'*Hurt* ... You ripped my guts out!' Constantine shot back in a raw explosion of emotion that silenced her. 'How would you have felt? I thought we were getting close, and then all of a sudden I find out you're not even the person I thought you were...and then...*Theos*...I wake up with the most incredible hangover and I know that you still are...'

'You *still* think I'm a bitch?'

Constantine threw his arms wide in furious frustration. 'Of course not! That's not what I meant!'

'It's what it sounded like,' Rosie mumbled chokily as she stalked over and began pulling out drawers.

'Last night I thought you had to hate me and I haven't had much practice at talking about feelings. I attack first. I couldn't think straight until this morning and then when I got up you'd vanished...'

Hearing the ragged, raw strain in his deep, dark drawl, Rosie ached but refused to look at him, her hands shaking as she mounded clothes willy-nilly into a huge pile. He didn't love her but he certainly had loved and respected her father.

In the dragging silence his mobile phone buzzed.

'Go on... answer it!' Rosie hissed nastily over one shoulder.

With a strangled, driven imprecation, he did so. Rosie listened but she didn't even recognise the language. It wasn't Greek or French... And then she heard him say 'Cinzia' as clear as a bell and sheer murderous rage just exploded like a blazing fire-ball inside her. Scrambling up, she launched herself at him, ripped the mobile phone from his hand and plunged it into the carafe of cold water beside the bed.

'You can talk to Cinzia when I'm gone, not before!' she condemned strickenly. 'I hope the two of you rot in hell... I hope her husband catches you with her and kills you!'

As she spun away again, shaking and trembling like a leaf in a high wind, a pin-dropping silence thundered all around her.

'Cinzia and I split up years ago. We're still friends,' Constantine said almost conversationally. 'If I allowed Anton and Thespina to assume it was an ongoing affair, it was only because it became very embarrassing to be presented with marriageable young women every time I went to dine with them.'

Rosie blinked and sucked in a slow, steadying breath.

'Both of them were painfully keen for me to marry and settle down. I wasn't interested. Cinzia made a good cover story and they stopped lining up blind dates for me.'

In horror, Rosie surveyed the mobile phone sunk at the foot of the glass water container.

'There's no need for you to be jealous of Cinzia. That was over a long time ago.'

Intense mortification engulfed her. 'I'm not jealous!'

'If you say so...' Disturbingly, a thread of tender amusement softened Constantine's response. 'But I do feel that I ought to point out that every time I have had anything to do with another woman you have seen her off with the efficiency of a hit man!'

'I was pretending to be a wife... *just* pretending.'

'I don't want you to pretend any more. If you walk out that door, I'll feel like my life's going to end ...'

Stiffening in disbelief, Rosie brushed a wavering hand across her damp cheeks and twisted round. She saw him through a haze of tears. His compelling dark golden eyes were fixed on her with such intense hunger and hope, she trembled.

'I know you still think you're in love with Maurice,' Constantine framed hoarsely. 'But I think you'll grow out of that if I'm patient. I can't face losing you. I tried to last night and all I ended up with was this sense... this knowing that really nothing else mattered as long as I still had you ...'

Rosie licked her dry lips and waited, fingers rolled into feverish fists because she was so desperate to fling her arms round him but she wanted to hear the words first.

Constantine breathed in slowly like a non-swimmer about to plunge into a deep pool without a lifebelt. 'I love you like crazy—'

Rosie hurled herself at him. 'I'm not in love with Maurice, I'm in love with you ... and I'm sorry I hurt you but I couldn't stand for you to want to stay married to me just because Anton was my father,' she gasped out in a confiding rush, fingers flexing joyously over wide, strong shoulders she had never thought to explore again and lingering in a deeply possessive hold.

He closed his arms round her so tightly, she could barely breathe. 'Didn't you realise that I loved you last night? Why do you think I got so damn drunk?'

'I never even dreamt that I could affect you like that.'

'And now that you know you're not going to allow me to forget it.' Constantine tipped her head up and searched her eyes for confirmation of what he so badly wanted to believe. A brilliant smile drove the last of the tension from his dark features and his gaze gleamed possessively over her.

'The first time I saw you it was like hitting a wall at two hundred miles an hour. I lost my head when I found you at Anton's house because you were the very last woman I wanted to find there. I wanted you to be mine and I wouldn't admit that to myself.'

'I really got on your nerves at the start.' Rosie's fingers were happily engaged in unknotting his silk tie and yanking it off.

'You wouldn't let me ignore you and then I began making excuses for you...didn't you notice that?' Helpfully he detached himself long enough to shrug free of his jacket. It fell unnoticed to the floor for they only had eyes for each other.

'Excuses?' Rosie queried, unbuttoning his shirt with a frown of concentration.

'On your behalf, I began to come up with all sorts of understandable reasons for you to have ended up as an older man's mistress.'

'Like that Maurice was a bad influence who had taken advantage of me, that I was in love with him and flung myself at Anton in despair,' Rosie recounted for herself, a faintly dazed light in her eyes as she marvelled at her own lack of perception and dragged his shirt down his arms and off. 'You were making terrific excuses for me even before we ended up in bed.'

'You didn't notice...I did,' Constantine confided, watching with slightly bemused eyes as Rosie embarked on his belt. 'Theos...it really shook me that you could have that much effect on my brain. And I was eaten up with jealousy of Maurice. You never shut up about him. Every time I thought I might be getting somewhere with you, *he* came into it again.'

'He's my best friend and there's never been the tiniest spark between us. You misjudged him,' Rosie scolded, gaining in confidence by meteoric degrees as she spread a smile of unconcealed admiration over Constantine's bare chest.

'Misjudged him?' Constantine shuddered as Rosie moved on to more physical ways of demonstrating her love and appreciation. She muttered a distracted explanation about Maurice's sister, Lorna, and her unfortunate experience with the journalist she had fancied. It became very involved and eventually petered out entirely.

She ran blissful hands across his hair-roughened chest and down over his long, powerful thighs before sliding them up to the hard bulge straining at his zip. He groaned out loud as she let her fingers shape him. And then he grabbed her up to him and plundered her mouth with hungry need. They fell backwards on the bed. He ripped her clothes off. This time Rosie helped and returned the favour...

A long while later, they were wrapped together in a gloriously happy haze of mutual satisfaction and the sheer wonder of loving each other, an abstracted frown clouded Rosie's brow. 'There's just one thing I don't understand... *rabbits*? Why did Dmitri tell me you were talking about rabbits?'

Constantine shifted a little tautly and faint colour darkened his blunt cheekbones. 'There are two whole crates of them downstairs.'

'Excuse me?' Rosie stared down at him.

'Those Sylvac rabbits you collect... you remember that one I broke? Last week I got on the phone and spoke to a dealer and he put the word out, and you are now the owner of probably the most expensive collection of ceramic rabbits in the world today.'

A delighted grin illuminated Rosie's face. 'That's so sweet, Constantine. You must have been really desperate to impress me.'

'You're such a diplomat, Rosie.' His dark golden eyes glittered over her and a slanting, wicked smile curved his mouth. 'I'll be equally tactless. When are you planning to tell me exactly what I do in these fantasies of yours?'

Rosie went pink. 'I don't want to shock you.'

'Did I say a word when my mobile phone went swimming?' Reaching up to tug her insistently down to him again, Constantine kissed her breathless. An almost soundless little sigh of contentment escaped her. She wondered how much he would enjoy playing a gangster...